CRAZY FOR YOU

A LODGE SERIES NOVEL

J.H. CROIX

This is a work of fiction. Names, characters, businesses, places, events and incidents are either the products of the author's imagination or used in a fictitious manner. Any resemblance to actual persons, living or dead, or actual events is purely coincidental.

Cover design by Najla Qamber Designs

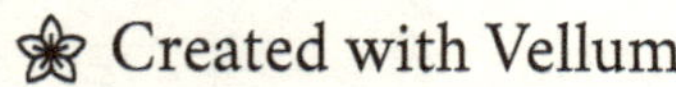 Created with Vellum

To starting over... and over and over again.

Sign up for my newsletter for information on new releases!

http://jhcroixauthor.com/subscribe/

Follow me!
jhcroix@jhcroix.com
https://www.bookbub.com/authors/j-h-croix
https://www.facebook.com/jhcroix
https://www.instagram.com/jhcroix/

Sawyer Hamilton gritted his teeth and swore under his breath as he climbed the stairs into the hospital. Searing pain shot through his knee when he cleared the last step. He swallowed his next muttered curse and navigated through the revolving door, not an easy thing to do with a bum knee. Once he made it inside, he paused and glanced around. He'd refused his brother's offer to accompany him here and for the moment, he temporarily regretted it. He was tired of being in pain and not in the mood to find his way around a labyrinth. The hospital in Diamond Creek, Alaska was much larger than he'd anticipated with several long hallways branching off the main entrance. He scanned the signs, looking for anything that would tell him where the laboratory was. He finally saw the sign indicating he needed to find his way to the third floor.

He limped into the elevator, relieved no one else happened to be waiting. The elevator whispered to a stop, and he stepped off. When he saw another sign for the laboratory pointing down a long hallway, he swore again and limped his way there. Sitting down with a sigh, he leaned his head against the wall and waited, doing his damnedest to ignore the pain radiating from his leg. While he waited, a few other people rotated in and out of the waiting room. He could feel the curious gazes on him, but he ignored them. He was accustomed to feeling strong, the opposite of how he'd been feeling since he'd had a close encounter with an IED in Iraq. He'd been lucky all in all, yet it didn't change the fact he was about sick to death of limping around. He'd rather be invisible right about now.

"Sawyer Hamilton?"

At the sound of his name, he glanced up—straight into a pair of breathtaking blue eyes. He stared at the woman standing across the room. Aside from her stunning eyes, she had a heart-shaped face with a creamy complexion and rosy cheeks. Combined with her almost black hair, she was plain gorgeous. He must've stared a beat too long because the woman to whom the eyes belonged arched a brow. He stood. "That's me."

The woman pushed off the shoulder she'd been leaning against the doorframe and stepped to him. "Violet Carter," she said, holding a hand out.

Sawyer closed his palm around hers and felt a jolt of electricity race up his arm and radiate through his body. Violet had a firm, no-nonsense handshake. "Follow me," she said briskly as she turned and walked through a door that led to, guess what, another hallway.

He took a deep breath and followed, his eyes drawn to the swing of Violet's hips as she walked ahead of him. She was all curves, more so because she was on the shorter side. If the top of her head reached his chin, he'd be surprised. With him roughly an inch above six feet, that didn't mean she was particularly short. Her generous hips swayed with each step, along with her almost-black hair swinging in a ponytail. Her hair was tied back with a bright purple ribbon to match her purple scrubs. She glanced over her shoulder and paused to wait for him.

"Sorry. I walk too fast sometimes," she said with a rueful smile when he reached her side.

"Don't think it's you walking too fast. It's me gimping along behind you," he said wryly.

Her eyes crinkled with her smile. "You're not too gimpy, although I bet it feels like it to you. Come on, we're almost there," she said, tucking her hand in the crook of his elbow. Somehow, she managed to take just enough weight off his bad side for the pain to ease slightly.

He didn't know what to think about his body's reaction to Violet. All she'd done was curl her hand around his elbow and another jolt of electricity zinged through him. He hadn't given a thought to a woman in months—not since his accident. Before that, well, it was safe to say his life hadn't allowed much time for relationships, casual or otherwise. He'd been on active duty as a Navy SEAL for the last ten years. That meant confidential missions all over the world and frequent travel. When he was home for visits with family, all he wanted was to turn his brain off. He'd had a few casual relationships here and there, but since he'd gotten too close for comfort with an IED, he'd gone through one round of surgeries and was on indefinite medical leave. He'd shattered his femur so badly, it had taken six hours for them to piece it together with steel pins. His femur was healed now, but a few bits of shrapnel had been missed in the emergency surgery, so he was finally cleared to get those removed. While the pain was relentless, he'd been advised his recovery after this would be swift compared to what he'd been through so far.

Despite that, his leg would never be the same again. He'd sustained too much damage. He was out of sorts and the last thing on his mind was any woman. Yet, Violet's mere presence caught his body's attention.

Violet paused to open a door and gestured him through. "Have a seat," she said, pointing to a chair beside a counter.

Sawyer hated how accustomed he'd become to the feel of medical offices and labs. This room felt like any of the many medical labs he'd visited in the last few months. The space held a sterile feeling with its white walls and gleaming tile floors. Everything was white and stainless steel. Violet closed the door and sat down in front of him, lifting a clipboard off of a wheeled table beside her. She scanned whatever was clipped there before looking up at him. "Looks like they have you scheduled for surgery in Anchorage next week. We're just doing some preliminary tests for your surgery. Any questions before I draw your blood?"

He looked over into her eyes—a deep, translucent blue that he could lose himself in—and lost track of what she said. Her eyes stood out against her creamy complexion and dark hair. She arched a brow. "Sawyer? You with me here?"

"Oh right. Uh, nope, no questions. Let's just get this done."

Those gorgeous blue eyes scanned his face, and he felt as if she could see right through him to the man who was weary from pain and stumbling through how to accept the reality of physical limitations for the first time in his life. He closed his eyes, shuttering himself the only way he could.

"Okay. Let's get this done. Are you left handed or right handed?" she asked, her voice matter of fact but warm.

"Right. Why do you ask?" he countered, opening his eyes again. He'd been in and out of doctor's offices and the hospital for months, and no one had bothered to ask that question.

She reached over and lowered the arm to the chair on his left side, patting it for him to rest his arm there. "So I can draw blood from your non-dominant side. No sense in making your strong side sore. I promise I do my best to make it painless, but there's always a little residual soreness. Can't stab you and have it be totally pain free," she said with a grin.

"You call it stabbing?" he asked with his own grin. The desire to smile came infrequently of late, so it was nice to banter about something silly like this.

Violet rolled her eyes as she busied herself getting a few vials out and carefully lining up her instruments on the small table at her side. "I'm teasing. It's not really stabbing, just a poke with a needle. I guess not a lot of people want to be a phlebotomist, but I did. I had leukemia when I was a little girl. I had my blood drawn so often I got really particular about whether they were doing a good job. I decided I might as well do it myself," she said with a shrug as she turned to him again.

She was so lively and warm, it was hard to imagine her being sick. Just considering it made his heart clench. "Are you...?" He trailed off, realizing he'd been about to get more curious than he should.

"Still sick? Nope. Most children diagnosed with leukemia experience a full recovery. I've been clear for years, but I spent plenty of time in the hospital before that. I'm healthy as a horse now," she said with a wink. "Anyway, onto you. We have to do the obvious dance now."

"The obvious dance?" he asked, having no idea what she meant.

"The dance where I ask you incredibly obvious questions to confirm who you are and why you're here. You know, all the stuff that would be a complete nightmare if we mixed it up."

"Oh right. Sawyer Hamilton, date of birth October 11th, 1983."

Violet smiled slowly. "You've done this a few times. Okay, the paperwork says you're here for preoperative testing for knee surgery scheduled next week. Is that correct?"

"Sure is," he replied, unable to keep from returning her slow smile.

"We're done with the obvious dance." She shifted to all business. In seconds, she'd prepped his arm and drawn blood so quickly, he barely noticed.

As she carefully labeled the vials of blood, he rolled his sleeve down. "Well, that was the most painless blood draw I've ever had."

He could see her lips curl in a smile from the side. She set the vials in a rack and spun in her chair to face him. "I do my best. Trust me, I became a discerning patient when it came to getting my blood drawn. Try being a kid and getting poked with needles all the time. I hated it and especially hated when people were careless about it."

"You set a high bar," he said with a slow nod. He couldn't quite believe he was bantering about getting his blood drawn. It wasn't just bantering, it was flirting and he damn well knew it. At the moment, he didn't care to ponder how much he was enjoying it.

"So, I can't say I've seen you around town before. Are you from Diamond Creek?" she asked.

He shook his head. "Nope. I'm visiting my brother, Gage Hamilton. He owns Last Frontier Lodge…" He paused and gestured vaguely in the direction of the lodge. "I, uh, I'm on leave from active duty until they clear me. I was born here, but our parents moved away when I was a kid. Gage came back to renovate the lodge our grandparents owned. Then my brother Garrett moved here and my sister Jessa too. I figured I'd rather be laid up here with family nearby than anywhere else."

Violet smiled. "Oh, I know who your family is! Can't say I know them well, but I've met them all in passing one way or another. It's kinda hard not to eventually know everyone around here."

"Are you what they call local?"

She threw her head back with a laugh, and his whole body tightened. Holy hell. With those amazing blue eyes and her dark hair, when her cheeks flushed it sent electricity spinning through his veins.

"I suppose I'm local now, but I'm not from here. I think you have more cred than me since you were born here. I moved here from New York City about a year and a half ago. I wanted a change of pace, and I definitely found it here."

"I'd say. So you like it here?"

"I love it. Diamond Creek's small, but with all the tourists, there's great shopping, great restaurants and plenty to do. Lots of people complain about the cost of living here, but it's hard to beat New York City for that." She grinned again, and he was starting to learn if he wanted to improve his mood and take his mind off of the endless weary loop of pain, all he needed to do was spend more time with her.

"I'll bet," he finally managed to reply when she arched a brow again.

He sat there, not wanting to leave and wondering how to drag this appointment out.

* * *

VIOLET SAT THERE GRINNING like a fool and wondering how to keep Sawyer Hamilton in her office a little longer. Foolish didn't quite capture how she felt. She'd looked across the waiting room at him and her heart had skipped a beat. Sawyer was all kinds of sexy with his chocolate brown hair, smoky gray eyes and body to die for. It didn't surprise her in the slightest to learn he was military. The man's body looked as if it had been carved from stone. She could tell he was in some pain, which bothered her more than it should. She dealt with patients experiencing pain all the time. It wasn't that she didn't feel empathy for all of them, even the cranky, irritable patients who took out their frustration on her. Yet, with Sawyer, she wanted to hold him close and make the pain melt away. He held a sense of weariness that hit her right in her heart.

You just think he's sexy as hell.

Maybe so, but that's not all.

She caught herself about to shake her head, a response to her internal conversation with herself. She needed to stop drooling over this guy and be professional. Even if it seemed like there was a little buzz between them, Sawyer was here to get his blood drawn, not to have her fantasize about him. She looked over at him again. His eyes locked onto her. The color was like nothing she'd ever seen—the sky on a stormy day, smoky with flashes of silver. A shiver raced through her, followed with heat rolling through her in a wave.

For a moment, she was frozen, so startled at the intensity of her body's reaction to nothing more than a look from him that she couldn't move. This was so *not* her. This time she actually shook her head, standing abruptly as she did. She started to walk swiftly and came to a screeching halt, the screech part in her mind of course, when she heard him stand carefully and then mutter a curse.

She turned back, her heart giving a little squeeze when she saw the tight lines on his face. "I didn't mean to rush you. Are you okay?"

His smoky gaze met hers again, but this time she braced herself. He straightened, and her eyes just had a mind of their own, greedily following the line of his strong shoulders and along his muscled chest. Dear God, even his hands were strong and sexy. The back of one palm was marked with a scar, while a black tattoo curled around his wrist in bold strokes. He cleared his throat, and her eyes whipped up, her cheeks heating instantly. If he noticed she was all but eating him up with her eyes, he didn't let on. He gave his knee a careful shake and then took a step toward the door, grimacing. "Damn!" His muffled exclamation gave her heart another squeeze.

"Are you...?" Her question trailed off when his eyes met hers.

"I'm fine. Hate to admit it, but I suck at dealing with pain. I'm not willing to take those damn meds that make my brain fuzzy, so I'm getting through it with lots of swearing. It really only hurts when I go from sitting to standing and vice versa. Hard to believe, but I'm doing a hell of a lot better than I was. I was clunking around in a cast for my shattered femur for two months. All that's left are a few bits of shrapnel. They're the pain equivalent of mosquitoes, relentless and annoying as hell."

She bit her lip and caught herself twirling the end of her ponytail, one of her dead giveaway nervous habits. She resisted the urge to ask him all kinds of questions about how he got injured. She had enough sense to know injuries involving shrapnel happened only in certain situations, but now certainly wasn't the time or place to pelt her questions at him. She dropped her ponytail and next thing she knew, she was fiddling with the pen she kept in her pocket. Sawyer closed the distance between them, his steps smoother now. He rested his hand on the counter beside the door and looked over at her. Meanwhile, she seemed to be stuck again. He was close enough she could feel the heat emanating from him. Her belly did a slow flip and her pulse skittered wildly.

His words fell into the quiet, weighted moment. "Don't suppose you'd help me find my way out."

"Of course. Come on." Without thinking, she slipped her hand in the crook of his elbow and gave him a gentle tug. "I'll make sure we get you all the way to the front entrance."

He pushed off the counter and gamely walked alongside her. His limp wasn't too bad once he got going. Questions spun through her mind. She wanted to know everything about him all at once. They made their way down the long hallway upstairs and into the elevator. She thought perhaps she should ease her hand free from where she'd curled it around his arm, but she didn't want to stop touching him. She savored the subtle flex of his muscles under her grip. He didn't seem inclined to tug free and simply leaned a shoulder against the side of the elevator, angling his body toward hers.

When he looked down, his smoky gaze locking with hers, the space inside the elevator felt suddenly crowded. Her breath hitched and heat rolled through her. His eyes searched her face, almost as if he was looking for something. He lifted his free hand and slid it through the end of her ponytail where it rested on her shoulder. His fingertip landed on her collarbone and traced up her neck, his touch a trail of fire. His eyes had dropped down and lifted again. Whatever he saw in hers, he gave a subtle nod and dipped his head.

His lips came against hers in a soft brush. She heard her breath come out in a gasp as if from a distance. She was so stunned this was happening, she couldn't quite believe it. Another soft brush of his lips and then he turned more fully toward her. In a flash, she knew the man he was—strong, confident and so damn sexy he made her knees weak. He threaded his free hand in her hair, while she hung onto his arm as if it was keeping her from drowning. His hand slid to cup the nape of her neck, and he fit his mouth over hers. On her next gasp, his tongue swept inside, and she forgot everything else, but...the feel of his hard, hot body against hers, his tongue sliding in a slow tease with hers and a wild, thrumming need racing through her so hard and fast, her knees buckled.

By the time he drew away, she was surprised she hadn't melted right then and there. She opened her eyes to find his staring back at her. He looked as stunned as she felt. The elevator came to a stop, shuddering slightly. He turned smoothly, using the railing along the inside of the elevator to support him. The doors whooshed open, and several people stood there waiting to step inside.

Flustered beyond belief, Violet managed to walk beside Sawyer out of the elevator and to the front entrance. The hum of the hospital was distant with people walking briskly here and there, while all she could think about was the fact he'd kissed her nearly senseless in the elevator. When they reached the revolving door, he looked down at her. A subtle flush crested his cheekbones. He searched her face again, while she tried to think of what to say.

Just as she was about to speak, someone called her name. She spun around to see one of the ER nurses waving for her. "Did you get your page?" the nurse called out.

Violet looked to Sawyer. He was already pulling his arm free from her hand. "Looks like you need to go. I'll get out of your way," he said quickly, stepping into the revolving door as it spun by.

"Good luck with your surgery," she said abruptly before the door whisked around.

He flashed a grin and gave a small wave. She turned and hurried away.

CHAPTER 2

Sawyer laid down his cards, a straight flush, and looked across the table at Garrett. Garrett threw his head back with a laugh and took a drag of beer. "Thought I had you there. I forgot how good your poker face is. You looked bored as hell," Garrett said with a chuckle as he gathered the cards up from the table.

Sawyer shrugged. "Looking bored is my go to with you. You should know that by now," he offered with a grin.

Garrett set the cards aside and leaned back in the booth. Garrett was one of Sawyer's older brothers and had followed Gage, the oldest of all of the Hamilton siblings, to Diamond Creek. At the moment, they were enjoying yet another dinner in the lodge restaurant and Garrett, as usual, wanted to play cards. Garrett arched a dark brow and cocked his head to the side, his blue eyes sharp on Sawyer. "Maybe I should, but you have to agree we've hardly seen you for the last few years. I forgot. I won't forget again," he said with a wink.

Sawyer chuckled. "Didn't imagine you would."

Garrett's gaze sobered. "It's good to have you here, man. Really good."

Sawyer felt his chest tighten, but he breathed through it. Aside from his gimpy leg, it was damn good to be with his brothers and sisters and then some. He'd followed Gage into the Navy and then the SEAL's, but Gage had retired from the military a few years back. He'd wanted out while he was still young enough to start something new. He'd done a bang up job resurrecting their grandparents' old ski lodge back from abandonment and turning it into a world class resort again. He'd also managed to fall in love and have a baby while he was at it. Even though Sawyer and Gage hadn't been on the same SEAL team, it hadn't been the same for Sawyer since Gage retired. He'd felt pangs of loneliness. Somehow, just knowing another family member was out there with him had made it easier.

Their family was close, always had been, so it was an incredible relief to have them to fall back on since his injury. He'd thought about staying with their parents down in Bellingham, Washington. With Gage, Garrett, and Jessa here in Alaska, Sawyer had elected to come here. His parents visited often, along with their sister Becca who lived in Seattle. Aside from his annoyance with his injuries, Sawyer was glad to be back with his family. He met Garrett's eyes and nodded. "Really good to be here. I just gotta get through that surgery, and I can breathe easy again."

"You still planning to return to your team?" Garrett asked, his perceptive gaze on Sawyer.

Sawyer started to say yes, but he paused. Truth was, he didn't know anymore. He'd spoken at length with his commanding officer who'd made it clear there was no certainty Sawyer would be medically cleared at all. He'd likely be able to live without pain and function well, yet the rigorous physical requirements of being a SEAL couldn't be met without near-perfect physical condition. His commanding officer had looked right at him and told Sawyer he could let his retirement be his own decision or someone else's. Sawyer was still mulling that one over.

He leaned back and idly twirled his empty beer bottle in his hand. "Honestly, I dunno. There's a high likelihood I won't be medically cleared for active duty, not as a SEAL team member that is. I've got time to decide on my own, so I'm taking it."

Garrett nodded slowly, relief evident in his eyes. "It's your call, but I'd be lying through my teeth if I didn't tell you we'd all be happy to see you home."

Sawyer nodded. "I'll keep that in mind." That's all he was willing to say, not because he didn't want to talk to Garrett about it, but because he had to sort it out in his own head.

Garrett started to say something else when the swinging door to the restaurant's kitchen opened and Garrett's wife stepped through with two plates in her hands. Delia tossed a smile in Sawyer's direction before beaming at Garrett. With her honey gold hair, blue eyes and warm personality, she was a contrast to Garrett's dark hair, angular features and sharp edges. Whenever Sawyer saw them together, he tended to feel as if he was interrupting. Garrett was beyond head over heels in love with Delia and bordering on sappy. Delia set the plates down in front of them and dropped a kiss on Garrett's cheek, only to get dragged onto his lap. "Oh no you don't," Garrett said as she laughed and started to wiggle out of his arms. "You've been working too much lately. Gage already told me you're not even supposed to be working tonight. Take this off..." He paused as he swiftly untied her apron and tugged it over her head. "...and eat with us," he finished.

Delia flushed and looked to Sawyer. "Was he always this pushy?"

Sawyer grinned. "Always. This time, he's right though. Take a break and eat with us."

They were at the ski lodge's restaurant where his siblings and their respective families and friends often gathered. With Gage and Marley residing at the lodge in their private quarters and the amazing food, it was an easy choice for them to casually land here. Gage had insisted Sawyer stay in his own suite at the lodge, so he'd quickly discovered the major bonus of awesome food all day long if he wanted it. As the restaurant's chef and manager, Delia made that magic happen.

Delia climbed off of Garrett's lap, snatching her apron off the floor. "Give me five minutes."

After she disappeared into the kitchen

again, Sawyer looked over at Garrett. "Delia's the best thing that's ever happened to you."

"Don't need to tell me. Trust me, everything's better because of her."

"I can see that. If you'd told me a few years ago that you, of all people, would close shop on your high rollin' law practice in Seattle and fall in love with a single mother, I seriously wouldn't have believed it," Sawyer said with a slow shake of his head. "Damn happy for you. Damn happy for all of you. Can't believe it, but it's been like dominoes. Once Gage fell, the rest of you got in line."

Garrett winked. "Yup. You're next."

Sawyer rolled his eyes. He'd already had to listen to Becca carry on about how he needed to settle down when he'd visited her in Seattle. "Right. Doubt that. Seeing as I'm gimpy as hell, now is definitely not the time to be looking for love."

"It's the perfect time," a voice said from over his shoulder.

Sawyer glanced back to find Gage approaching the table. Gage hooked his hand over a chair near their booth and swung it to sit at the end. He shared Sawyer's brown hair and gray eyes. As with Garrett, Gage had mellowed considerably since his relocation to Diamond Creek. Sawyer had worried about him after Gage's close friend had died while they were on a mission. Yet, Gage had rebounded after returning to the place they'd all been born and finding something that mattered to him.

Gage nabbed one of the sweet potato fries off of Sawyer's plate and grinned.

"Dude, it's the opposite of a perfect time," Sawyer said, moving his plate further away from Gage's hands and taking a bite of his salmon burger. Despite his outward comments, his mind instantly conjured Violet—her deep blue eyes and the subtle flush on her cheeks after he kissed her.

Unrepentant, Gage grabbed another fry, gobbling it up before replying. "How would you know? As far as I know, you haven't been in love. So take it from me, gimpy's perfect. It means you won't be all badass and serious because you kinda can't pull that off when you're limping around. Makes you nicer. Plus, love will improve your mood."

Garrett almost choked on a sip of his beer and grabbed a napkin to wipe his chin. Sawyer just kept eating, almost in disbelief that he had not one, but two brothers lecturing him on love.

Garrett's eyes flicked from Gage to Sawyer.

"Wow, I was kinda teasing him, but I think you're serious."

Gage shrugged. "Sure. I'm all about anything that will keep him here." He snagged another fry and chewed thoughtfully. "I'll talk to Marley. She'll talk to Ginger who knows everyone and we'll find someone for Sawyer."

Garrett started laughing, while Sawyer glanced between them, incredulous. He expected a little pushing from his sisters about things like this, but not his brothers. It was beyond ridiculous. He could *not* deal with Gage recruiting friends to manage his love life. "Man, you'd better not try your hand at matchmaking with me. I'm not arguing against your point. Obviously, you two have found love, light and happiness, but let me be, okay?"

"Oh, I'm not the matchmaker. I'll put a bug in Ginger's ear, and she'll be all over it," Gage said with a wink.

He was referring to Ginger Nash, whom Sawyer had gotten to know in the few weeks he'd been staying at the lodge. Ginger was married to Cam who worked at the lodge with Gage. Sawyer might not know Ginger particularly well, but he knew beyond a shadow of a doubt she'd be like a dog with a bone on this. She'd already badgered him about playing baseball next year even though he'd pointedly explained he didn't know if he'd even be here. He did not need his family and their friends trying to set him up.

Violet passed through his thoughts again. Now if Ginger wanted to set him up with Violet, that would be more than fine. Violet with those eyes he got lost in, her wry sense of humor, and a kiss that almost knocked him over. He hadn't meant to kiss her the other day in the elevator, but he did because it was all he'd wanted right then and there. Since then, he'd replayed that kiss quite a few times and wondered when he'd see her again. With her job as specific as it was, he couldn't exactly drop by unless he needed his blood drawn again. He wanted to see her badly enough, he might schedule an appointment just for the hell of it.

VIOLET ROLLED her car to a stop and climbed out. A salty breeze gusted her way and sent a shiver through her. Mornings in Alaska were always cool, even at the height of the summer. She loved the crisp early morning air and often headed to the beach for a walk as she had this morning. Kachemak Bay spread out in view before her with mountains rising tall out of the water on the far side. Violet still chuckled when she remembered seeing the job posting for a phlebotomist here. She'd pulled up a map of Alaska and zeroed in on Diamond Creek. The town's website had plenty of spectacular photos, but she'd assumed they were those once in a blue moon type of pictures. Then she'd moved here and quickly learned she was living in a postcard.

Diamond Creek was located in Southcentral Alaska on the Kenai Peninsula. The town was a tourist mecca for wilderness lovers, eco-tourists, arts lovers, and skiers. Despite it's small population due to its remote location in coastal Alaska, the town had great food and shopping if you discounted the high prices. Being born and raised in New York City meant Violet was accustomed to high prices, so she didn't find it any different. She loved the sense of community and the feeling of living on the edge of the wilderness. This part of Alaska offered the amazing combination of the ocean and the mountains at the same time, along with plenty of wildlife. The view was so ridiculous, she almost laughed just now. Sun fell in shafts through the clouds, striking sparks on the surface of the bay. Boats were heading out of Otter Cove Harbor, the town's picturesque harbor tucked into its namesake cove.

After a bracing breath of air, Violent turned and walked to the small coffee truck. Red Truck Coffee was located at the corner leading into the harbor parking lot and did a brisk business until snow fell. Whenever she went for a morning walk at the beach, she stopped here before heading up to the hospital. It wasn't even six in the morning yet, but there was already a short line. Those headed out to fish for the day stopped by here before they hopped on their boats.

Violet glanced around as she waited, but she didn't recognize anyone. It was late summer and high time for tourist season, so on any given day, half the people she saw were visitors. She loved that she was getting settled enough to feel like she was part of the community here and not a visitor from a strange land. Coming from New York, she'd felt a bit out of place at first. When she reached the front of the line, she glanced up and grinned. "Hey Cammi! Is there ever a day you're not here?" she asked.

Cammi looked up, a warm smile stretching across her face. "I get the whole winter off, so I make up for it all summer," she replied. Cammi owned and ran Red Truck Coffee. With her short honey brown hair in a pixie cut, bright blue eyes and tendency to dress in flowing skirts and blouses, Cammi seemed like a fairy to Violet. She also made amazing coffee.

Violet arched a brow. "That's nice and all, but it doesn't give you much time to enjoy the summer."

"Sure it does. I make coffee all morning and then have the rest of the day to myself. You only come by first thing, but I usually have someone else cover the truck in the afternoons. Anyway, the usual for you?" Cammi asked.

At Violet's nod, Cammi spun away and prepped Violet's usual shot in the dark. When she spun back, she slid the coffee across the counter and gave a wave to someone approaching from behind. "Hey Jessa! I see you finally persuaded Sawyer to spend a day out on the water."

A prickle of awareness raced up Violet's spine. She knew it was the Sawyer she thought before she even looked. She turned to the side to see Sawyer approaching beside Jessa Brooks, whom Violet knew to be his sister. Jessa shared Sawyer's chocolate brown hair, albeit with the addition of blonde streaks. Her silver-gray eyes were a softer shade than his. Seeing them side by side, it was impossible to miss the fact they were related.

Sawyer's eyes landed on Violet, and butterflies massed in her belly while heat suffused her. Her pulse lunged wildly, and her breath caught, all the while she fought to rein in her body's wild response to him. The last time she'd seen him, well the only time she'd ever met the man, he'd kissed her senseless in an elevator. In the two days since, she'd replayed that kiss a few too many times in her brain. She curled her hand around the bright red paper cup of coffee and tried to slow her galloping pulse. *You cannot be this gaga over him. You barely even know him. That kiss was just a weird fluke.* Sawyer's gaze held hers, and his mouth curled up at one corner. Her body didn't think that kiss was a fluke, no matter what her brain had to say about it. In fact, she'd like to kiss him again…and again…and again.

Violet suddenly realized she was staring. Big time. She tore her eyes away from Sawyer and looked to Jessa who was talking to Cammi now. She'd zoned out so hard over Sawyer simply existing in space with her she hadn't even noticed Jessa and Cammi were talking. *Bad, you've got it bad.*

"…Eli's taking us out for the day. I told him he has to make sure Sawyer brings home halibut and salmon," Jessa finished saying to Cammi before she turned to Sawyer and Violet.

"Sawyer," she said, gesturing to Cammi. "This is Cammi. Red Truck Coffee is hers and it's our go-to place all summer long. Eli would probably die without it." Jessa's eyes bounced to Violet. "Oh, and this is Violet, she…"

Sawyer cut in. "Nice to meet you Cammi," he said with a grin. His eyes flicked to Violet, and it was as if the air between them had its own humming current. She took a sip of her coffee, needing something to do. "I've actually had the pleasure of meeting Violet before. She holds the honor of the least painful blood draw I've ever had." He drew his words out and winked—winked!—at her.

Violet was quickly discovering Sawyer's smile was devastating, and it was clear he liked to tease. His eyes never left hers, while Cammi and Jessa both looked at her expectantly. This was the usual part of conversation where it was her turn to say something. Violet felt her cheeks heat and silently swore. With her pale complexion, even a mild blush turned her face rosy. This was no mild blush. Her mind flashed back to the feel of Sawyer's lips on hers in the elevator. *Not the time or place to go there.* Her taunting inner critic managed to shove her mind off that damn kiss. Then, her eyes collided with Sawyer's again. Like a stormy summer sky, his gaze locked with hers. He arched a brow, and her knees went weak.

Violet had no idea how much time had passed when Jessa spoke. "Oh, of course! You had to do those pre-op tests. I can't wait until that surgery's over. You'll be good as new soon," Jessa said, turning to Sawyer.

Something flickered in the back of his eyes, but it came and went so fast, Violet couldn't interpret it. "Here's hoping," Sawyer said with a wry grin.

Jessa looked between them curiously. "How've you been, Violet?" she asked. Violet couldn't say precisely how she'd met Jessa, but it was hard to live in Diamond Creek and not eventually encounter most locals in some fashion. She knew Jessa was married to Eli Brooks who ran Game to Fish, a local guiding business and high-end outdoor gear shop. If anything, Violet had probably met her there because when she'd first moved to Diamond Creek, she'd stocked up on winter gear at Eli's store.

Violet took another sip of coffee to distract herself from Sawyer. "Oh good. Just down here for a walk on the beach before I go to work. How about you?"

"Well, this is Eli's busiest time of year with charter trips and the store crazy busy. Ryan's working with him too, so they come home every night and collapse. Meanwhile, I'm busy at the gallery," Jessa said. Ryan was Eli's younger brother who lived with them. Jessa created gorgeous sets of painted furniture. Violet had purchased a small table from her when she was furnishing her apartment. Jessa must've ordered coffee while Violet had been gaga over Sawyer and turned to snag the cup of coffee Cammi slid across the counter. She looked over at Sawyer. "Did you say what you wanted?"

He finally turned away from Violet, and she breathed a small sigh of relief. Having those dreamy gray eyes of his on her sent her belly into somersaults. Somehow, Violet managed to get through a few more minutes of casual conversation. More customers showed up, so Violet said her goodbyes and started to walk back to her car. She'd just reached it when her skin prickled with awareness again. She glanced behind her to see Sawyer following her at a slower pace. His limp was subtle, but she knew from when she'd met him at the hospital that he might be in some pain. She was relieved at the slight delay in him reaching her, so she could steel herself not to go all fuzzy in her brain.

She took a slow breath, which went out in a whoosh the second he reached her and threw another one of his devastating grins her way. She gripped her cup of coffee as if she was holding on for dear life. He stopped in front of her and was quiet for a few beats, long enough she felt compelled to speak. "Um, did you need something?" she finally asked.

His eyes caught hers, his expression bemused. "I don't know if I need something, but I wanted to see you again."

Violet stared back at Sawyer, her brain trying to compute. "You want to see me?"

Uncertainty flickered in the back of his eyes before his lips curled in a wry smile. "I suppose so. Seeing as how you, well, you draw blood all day, I figured it's not like I'd have many chances to run into you. Unless I want to get my blood drawn for the hell of it."

She stood there, hanging onto her coffee

cup, and stared at him. She thought, maybe, he was trying to ask her out on a date. She hadn't been out on a date in, well, too long to remember. Maybe she was out of practice and that's why she couldn't seem to clarify what he meant. "You mean see me like a date? Or something else?"

He closed his eyes and chuckled softly, the sound sending a shiver over her skin. When he opened his eyes again, they landed on her and the air hummed to life around them. "Yes, I suppose that's what I meant. My surgery's next week, so maybe this weekend?"

Violet didn't know what to think, but there was no way in the world she'd say anything other than yes. Sawyer was too tempting, dangerously so. "Okay. The weekend's tomorrow. Do you mean Friday or Saturday?"

"Saturday. Not too late. Tell me where to find you, and I'll pick you up," he said.

Somehow she managed to tell him her address without stuttering. At which point, he asked for her number and entered it into his phone. Before she knew it, he'd tossed her another grin and turned to walk away. She looked past him to see Jessa talking with Eli and Ryan who must've driven up after she'd walked away. With a sharp shake of her head,

Violet climbed into her car and drove to work, wondering what the hell she was thinking. A kiss was one thing. A date was something else altogether.

She'd made a clear choice not to get too involved when it came to romance. It was a choice that helped her keep her sanity and guaranteed she wouldn't let anyone down the way she had once before. Once upon a time, she'd fancied herself in love. She'd even gotten engaged. She'd had all kinds of hopes and dreams, including children. Then, she'd learned one brutal truth about surviving childhood cancer. She couldn't have children. Many people who had cancer went on to live, long healthy lives and have their own children. But some survivor's lost their fertility, and she happened to be one of them.

That brutal truth had been followed by the next one, which was she'd fancied herself in love with someone for whom that was non-negotiable. To this day, she didn't know if she'd truly been in love because the rug had been ripped out from under her so fast. She'd had to say good bye to her own hopes and dreams of children and face the fact the man she thought loved her didn't love her enough to stick around. The losses were all tangled together, and together they'd been devastating. To this day, she had mixed feelings about being infertile. What she told herself intellectually didn't match up with how it felt.

She shook her head, physically trying to swat away worries about things she couldn't change. She'd moved on from her broken engagement and was all the stronger for it. But she'd decided she didn't want to force anyone to let go of that kind of dream, so she'd planned to skip the preliminaries and not worry about dating. Independence suited her fine.

Now, she'd just gone and said she'd meet Sawyer for dinner. She was out of her mind. She tried to tell herself it was just dinner, but that was a thing for her. She didn't do anything halfway. Never had, no matter how hard she tried.

CHAPTER 3

Sawyer leaned against the boat railing and stared into the distance. They'd spent most of the day on the water. He'd personally caught two silver salmon and one halibut. The size of the halibut had startled him with Eli guessing the single fish, which looked like a gigantic flounder, to weigh over one hundred and fifty pounds. All Sawyer knew was his arms had been plenty tired by the time they got the fish over the side of the boat. Jessa had been on his case for weeks since he'd arrived in Diamond Creek to go fishing. He'd only been avoiding it because he'd worried his injured leg would impede him. It hadn't really. Ryan had been a big help at the end when it came to getting the fish out of the water. For now, Sawyer was tired, but in the good way. He'd stayed busy enough as the day passed that the pain in his knee had faded from his mind. The power of a healthy distraction worked wonders.

A salty breeze came in gusts off the water. He watched the mountains on the far side of Kachemak Bay receding in the distance as the boat motored back toward Diamond Creek. His childhood memories of Diamond Creek were vague, although almost all were pleasant. He remembered their parents bringing them up for visits every summer, endless days of sunshine, and playing in the spruce forest surrounding the ski lodge with his siblings. Off and on over the years, Gage would mention he missed Alaska, but of them all, he was the only sibling old enough to remember being here full-time. Their parents had moved to Bellingham, Washington when Sawyer was two years old, so he certainly didn't remember living here. None of them had known their grandmother never sold Last Frontier Lodge when she closed it up after their grandfather died. It wasn't until she passed away that he and his siblings had collectively learned they inherited the lodge and the extensive wilderness surrounding it.

When Sawyer heard Gage planned to move here and renovate the lodge, he'd not given it much thought. He was out of the country on a classified mission at the time and had other things on his mind. Then, he'd visited and seen Gage happier than he'd been in years with the lodge thriving and busy. Right about now, with the ocean breeze gusting around him, the glorious view on all sides, and the first time in months he'd forgotten about his pain, Sawyer was thinking he'd say yes to staying here forever if it meant he could feel this sense of ease.

Violet came to mind—her clear blue eyes, black hair and curvy body all meshing to snatch his breath away. He hadn't been thinking much when he'd followed her to her car to ask her to dinner. All he'd known was he wanted a chance to see her again before he went under the knife. His mind spun back to the other night when Garrett and Gage had been teasing him about finding someone. He wasn't so silly as to think Violet could be that, but in the whopping two times he'd seen her, all he wanted was to see her again. He'd readily admit he could be a bit of a flirt when he had the time, but this thing with Violet didn't feel quite like that. Oh, he wanted to tease, but there was more underneath—that thrumming electricity that spun to life inside whenever she was near.

There was a loud splash, and he glanced over his shoulder to see a whale breaching in the bay nearby. He turned and walked to the other side of the boat, just as Jessa called to him. "Sawyer! You have to come look!"

"Right here, Jess," he replied as he leaned against the railing beside her.

Jessa glanced sideways and grinned. Her gray eyes were so similar to his, it was like looking in a mirror. Her chocolate brown hair was pulled up in a messy ponytail with tendrils escaping every which way. "Isn't it awesome here?" she asked over the rumble of the motor.

They both watched as the humpback whale's tail disappeared under the water, leaving a wake behind it. Sawyer paused to look toward Diamond Creek where the picturesque harbor was coming into view and the mountains were visible in the distance. "It's pretty damn awesome," he replied, glancing back to her.

Jessa looped her hand through his elbow and squeezed. "I'm so glad you're here. Please tell me you'll stay," she said, her eyes open and sincere.

Jessa was the winsome, sentimental sibling.

As the youngest, she was always the one who'd tried to smooth the edges of any argument. She'd generally been carefree, but she seemed happier and more grounded than Sawyer had ever known her to be since she'd found Eli. Sawyer looked over at her and shrugged. "Thinking about it. It's not as simple as just deciding to move here. I have to formally retire from the Navy and take care of things on that end. To say it's a bit of a life change is an understatement," he said with a chuckle. He refrained from extrapolating further on his mixed feelings about it. Knowing he may be facing a shift to admin duty didn't sit well with him, yet neither did the reality that the choice might be out of his hands.

Jessa nodded and looked out over the water, her gaze pensive. "I know. But you can. You said you were already cleared for medical retirement."

"I know. I know you want me to decide sooner rather than later, but let me get through this surgery first, Jess. Okay?"

Her eyes flicked to his again. After a moment, she nodded. "I'll try to be patient." She paused as if considering something, a subtle gleam entering her eyes. "You like Violet," she said firmly.

He should've known Jess would say something. Unlike Garrett and Gage, it didn't surprise Sawyer in the least to have her focusing on his love life. Even before she'd found Eli, she was all about everyone finding their happily-ever-after. He arched a brow and grinned. "Maybe so. I'm assuming that's okay with you."

Jessa nodded emphatically. "Absolutely! I don't know Violet too well, but everything I know about her is good."

He couldn't help but chuckle. Jessa was ever the optimist. Just as he was about to reply, the boat bounced against a wave in the choppy water, sending a splash of sea water right onto him and Jessa.

She burst out laughing and looked over at him with her hair dripping wet. "I bet you could use a towel, huh?"

Sawyer grinned and dragged his sweatshirt sleeve across his face. "Might help," he said with a chuckle.

"Jessa!" Eli called out from where he stood steering the boat.

Sawyer glanced his way to see a towel sailing through the air toward them. The second he caught it, another landed in Jessa's hands. By the time they'd quickly toweled off, they'd almost reached the harbor. Ryan and

Jessa kicked into motion putting gear away and prepping the boat. Sawyer helped along the way, although it annoyed him to no end to have to be careful about his leg.

After the boat was tied up, and Ryan expertly fileted all of the fresh catch at warp speed, Sawyer followed Eli's truck back to their home. Jessa and Eli lived on the opposite side of town from the ski lodge up a winding hill that offered a spectacular view of Kachemak Bay when it was daylight. Sawyer followed them inside, glancing around at the living room they entered with its cathedral ceiling and windows stretching from floor to ceiling. The living room transitioned into the kitchen toward the back with an island serving as a natural divider. Jessa promptly ordered Sawyer to sit down while she began prepping a salad. Ryan disappeared into his room to shower, while Eli started up the grill on the back deck. After a few minutes, Sawyer glanced to Jessa.

"I'm heading out to the deck. Need me to carry anything out?" he asked as he stood.

Jessa glanced to him, blowing her breath and expertly sending a loose lock of hair out of her eyes. "You need to…"

He narrowed his eyes, predicting she was

about to fuss over him. "Don't tell me to take it easy, Jess. Everything but one knee is in perfectly good condition."

She rolled her eyes. "Fine. Carry this out." She gave him a stack of plates and tossed some napkins on top.

Sawyer joined Eli on the deck who promptly handed him a beer while he turned salmon and halibut filets on the grill. Sawyer took a drag on his beer and sat down at the round wooden table on the deck. Of course, it was one of Jessa's creations, so it wasn't just a table. It was beautifully painted with lupine and fireweed. He idly traced along one of the flowers and looked up at Eli when he turned off the grill and sat down across from Sawyer.

"Nice place here," he commented.

Eli nodded and leaned back, running a hand through his light brown hair. "Thanks. Bought it for a steal when the original owners ran out of money to finish the place. Jessa gets all the credit for making it nicer. Before she moved in, it was pretty sparse," he said with a low laugh.

"That's Jessa," Sawyer replied with a grin. Though he'd spent most of his adult life out of the country on missions, whenever he'd been in one spot for more than a few months,

Jessa came to visit and was like a whirlwind. No matter what, she always left a place better than she found it. Even when he was living in temporary digs, which had pretty much been his life the last ten years or so, she was the one who made them comfy. Jessa called something out to Ryan, and Sawyer looked back to Eli. "It's nice to see how happy Jess is with you. Can't believe I'm saying this, but I'm glad her apartment in Seattle burned down."

Eli threw his head back with a laugh. When his green gaze landed on Sawyer's again, he shrugged. "That's only funny because everyone got out okay."

They were referencing a fire in Jessa's old apartment building in Seattle that led to her losing just about everything she owned. In a tailspin, she'd driven up to visit with Gage and Marley while she figured out what to do. She met Eli and ended up staying. Sawyer returned Eli's shrug. "So true." He sobered. "Seriously, it's good to know she's settled. She loves it here. You guys have a good thing going. Ryan's an awesome kid too."

As if on cue, Ryan strolled through the open sliding glass door. His brown hair was damp. He slouched into a chair beside Sawyer and glanced between Sawyer and Eli. "How long until we can eat?" he asked.

Eli grinned. "Any minute now. Fish is ready. Just waiting for Jessa."

Eli stood and walked to the sliding glass door, peering inside. Sawyer looked over just as Jessa stepped to the door, juggling a bowl of salad and a bottle of wine in her hands. Eli dipped his head and dropped a kiss on the side of her neck as he took the salad bowl from her. The moment was brief, but so intimate Sawyer felt he needed to look away. Ryan caught his eyes and sighed. "They're like that all the time. It's kinda embarrassing sometimes."

Sawyer almost choked on his beer. "Things could be worse," he finally managed.

Ryan nodded somberly. "I know. It's awesome to be here, so I can deal with it," he said earnestly.

Sawyer recalled that Eli had obtained guardianship of Ryan after Ryan ran away from home and showed up in Diamond Creek. He knew things hadn't been too smooth for Ryan with his and Eli's parents, but he didn't have all the details, so he simply nodded. Jessa reached the table, her cheeks slightly flushed, and set the wine down.

"Okay, guys. Let's eat," she announced,

swinging around and carrying over the platter of fish from the grill.

A while later, Sawyer drove back to the lodge. The entire day and evening had been just plain good. He certainly hadn't considered it at the time, but being on forced medical leave was giving him the first true down time he'd had in years. Being a Navy SEAL meant frequent travel, a rigorous training schedule, and limited breaks. He still had mixed feelings about what to do after his surgery, but he could easily be persuaded that taking the medical retirement option and moving to Diamond Creek would be a good choice. Internally, he was torn over that choice though.

He didn't like feeling physically limited. Yet, he knew he'd be damn lucky if he were cleared for active duty as a SEAL again. His leg had been torn up when the IED exploded. They'd done preliminary on site stabilization and surgery to reconstruct his shattered femur. This follow up procedure was to remove the remaining shrapnel. His lingering pain was from nothing more than a few pieces of shrapnel missed in the first round of surgery. He'd stuck with a modified conditioning routine to stay in shape, which by most standards was a grueling workout. Yet, for him, he didn't feel up to par and only hoped he might after the surgery.

As he rounded a curve in the road and Last Frontier Lodge came into view, Violet strolled into his thoughts again. He half-wondered if he'd been ridiculous to try to see her before his surgery. Yet, he didn't want to wait through the recovery afterward where he most certainly wouldn't be up to seeing much of anyone beyond his family before he saw her again. He was a terrible patient and he damn well knew it. He didn't know what it was about Violet, but he wanted to have a little more than a passing encounter with her. He wanted to see her cheeks flush and those gorgeous blue eyes lock onto him again. He didn't quite know what to think about it, but with her, it wasn't just that she called to him physically. It was that he'd felt comfortable with her. Of all the situations to feel comfortable with someone, getting his blood drawn had to rank as one of the least likely, if anything because it took place in the cold, sterile hospital lab.

Violet stood in front of the mirror and swiftly ran a brush through her hair. She'd spent far too much time worrying about what to wear and finally settled on jeans and a bright blue shirt that fell in a swinging swirl at her hips with a scoop neck held together by a small bow. Even though she had no idea where Sawyer planned to take her, anywhere they went in Diamond Creek could handle casual. Her dark hair shone from her ruthless brushing. Restless and annoyed with herself for even worrying about how she looked, she left it down and practically stomped out of the bathroom.

Aside from her quite purposeful choice not to pursue relationships, she most certainly hadn't missed the worrying part of it. Dating, of any kind, was annoying. The whole wondering what someone wanted and everything that went with it nearly drove her mad. She'd forgotten that part of it. She kept reminding herself not to read too much into this and to remember she needed to keep her cool.

Sawyer had texted earlier today and confirmed he'd be by to pick her up around six. Her apartment was the upper floor of an office building in downtown Diamond Creek. With it being mid-summer, it was still daylight and would be for hours longer. Her living room and kitchen occupied one large room with windows overlooking Harborside Road with Otter Cove Harbor and the bay visible in the distance. She walked to the windows and looked out over the view. She still hadn't gotten used to waking up to this everyday. She loved New York City where she'd grown up, but it was all hustle and bustle and no view to speak of beyond the city unless one counted Central Park and the Hudson River, which were both quite lovely but most definitely urban. Here in Diamond Creek, she felt like she was on the edge of the wilderness, and she truly was. Yet, she had all the comforts of great restaurants, plenty of touristy shopping and an interesting mix of people.

She saw a black truck roll to a stop in front of the building. It didn't surprise her in the slightest to see Sawyer step out. She hadn't been able to resist doing a bit of gossip reconnaissance about him. She might be newer in town than many residents, but she knew how to gather information. She'd managed to learn he was a Navy SEAL and on medical leave due to whatever happened to his leg. That information proved to be somewhat unreliable because she'd heard everything from him getting shot on a mission to being nearby when an IED exploded. Diamond Creek was small, despite its status as a tourist destination. Anyone who wasn't a tourist passing through couldn't land here without making a few waves and creating gossip. She'd learned that herself when she first moved here. Sawyer might not be planning to stay, but he wasn't a tourist. He had family who'd quickly established themselves in Diamond Creek and had the credibility of being born here and descended from an old family that used to practically run the town. In her casual queries about Sawyer, she'd learned his grandfather, who had passed away over twenty years ago, had once been the mayor of Diamond Creek.

To say the locals were curious about Sawyer was an understatement. She'd overheard one of the elementary school teachers, Becky Wright, gabbing on about how hot he was. Violet wholeheartedly agreed, but she refrained from announcing it to the world. As if on cue, there was a knock at her door. She strode to the door and swung it open before she chickened out. Because she was that close to chickening out and telling Sawyer something came up. Perhaps the mama moose and her two calves in the trees behind her apartment would've served as a good excuse. She'd thought of telling him she couldn't safely leave because they were napping by the front stairs. That had actually occurred last week, so it wouldn't have been a total lie.

Yet, she hadn't chickened out. She looked up at Sawyer, and heat raced through her. His silvery gaze met hers, and his mouth curled up at one corner. *Oh, Violet. What have you done?* Her sensible self asked the question when her belly did a slow flip and her pulse skittered wildly.

"Hey there," Sawyer said, his voice slightly gruff.

Damn. Even his voice was hot. Just rough enough it sent shivers over her skin whenever he spoke. After a few beats, she realized she was simply standing there. He arched a brow, which nudged her out of her daze.

"Hey!" Her greeting came out a bit too forcefully.

His smile stretched from one side to the other. "Ready to go?"

Violet spun around, calling over her shoulder as she did. "Yup! Let me grab my jacket and purse."

She snatched a lightweight fleece jacket off the hooks by the door and grabbed her purse. It was still fairly warm out at the moment, but she knew it would cool within hours. Summer in Alaska meant warm days and cool nights, so she'd learned to always have a jacket on hand. He stepped to the side as she reached the door, waiting while she locked up behind her. When she turned to face him, he was leaning against the wall with his hand tucked in one pocket, giving her the tiniest glimpse of his muscled abs. It's not like she'd been wondering whether he had a body to die for, but that little glimpse sent heat pooling in her low belly.

She couldn't find her words, so she quickly jogged down the stairs only to swear softly when she realized his knee wasn't up for jogging. She turned back and bit her lip. "Sorry. I'm always rushing."

He wasn't that far behind and cleared the last step with a shrug. "I'm not too slow. Give me a few weeks, and I'll be back on track."

He held the door for her, surprising her. She settled herself in the passenger seat and glanced around as he walked to the driver's side. His truck was simple and high end with plush leather seats and about every electronic feature she could imagine. He glanced over as he started it, a gleam in his eyes. "I was told to take you to Diamond Creek Brewery or the Boathouse. Seeing as I haven't been to either place, I'll let you decide. Or you can tell me somewhere else."

Violet grinned. "Ah. I see you've been given good advice. Aside from those two places, the only others I'd suggest would be Sally's or the lodge restaurant. I'm guessing you've had plenty of chances to eat at the lodge."

He let the steering wheel slide through his relaxed grip as he backed up. "Oh, I'm spoiled rotten at this point. Delia keeps us well fed. If you want to go there, we can, but..."

"Oh no. Let's go somewhere you haven't been. Let's go to the Brewery."

He grinned and arched a brow. "Tell me how to get there."

He needed to stop grinning. It did crazy thing to her insides. Her pulse had taken off at a full gallop, and her belly was doing somersaults. She managed to catch her breath and tell him where to go. From where she lived, Diamond Creek Brewery was only a short drive. She was usually a chatty person, but found herself quiet on the drive over there. She was too busy trying to get her body under control. Prior to taking one look at Sawyer and getting all flustered, she'd have said she wasn't one of those women who went gaga over any man. Even when she'd been engaged, she hadn't been bowled over. Oh, she'd had an active sex life and enjoyed having fun, but that was it. Since her engagement blew up and she'd had to come to terms with her infertility and decided not to pursue romance, she hadn't missed much of anything. Oh, she was close personal friends with her favorite vibrator, but that was about it.

Sawyer showed up for a routine blood draw, and her body had gone haywire. She spent the few minutes on the way to the Brewery thinking about the most boring things she could, specifically the lab reports she ran at the end of every week. By the time he pulled into a parking spot in front of the Brewery, her pulse was back to normal. Then, he went and grinned again.

Oh hell. This was a problem.

"Are you sure this is a restaurant?" he asked, gesturing toward the building in front of them.

Sawyer's question nudged her out of the weirdness in her brain, mostly because it sent her into a fit of laughter. Once she managed to catch her breath, she glanced over to find him patiently waiting for her to answer, a bemused smile on his face.

She looked ahead at the Brewery and could easily see why someone might wonder. Aside from the sign and the cars out front, there wasn't much to clue one in that the place housed a restaurant. It happened to be in an old refurbished plane hangar. The owners had left the outside of the building as it was. As such, all that was visible was a giant plane hangar with its corrugated steel walls and a single door leading inside from the parking area.

"I'm sure," Violet finally said. "Come on."

By the time she had her seatbelt unbuckled, Sawyer had reached the passenger side of the truck and was opening her door. She caught his eyes. "Do you do this all the time?" she asked.

"Get the door?"

At her nod, he closed the door behind her as she stepped out, turning to walk at her side before replying. "Usually do. Is that a problem?" he asked as they reached the restaurant door. He promptly held it open, his eyes almost daring her to oppose his action.

She pondered his question as she stepped into the crowded entryway. She didn't mind anyone getting the door for her, yet she was by nature, an independent person and had perhaps taken great strides to become even more independent the last few years. She adored her parents, but to say they were a tad overprotective after she'd had childhood leukemia was a massive understatement. By the time she was officially clear from cancer, she'd been ready to jump for joy and scream her lungs out and do all the crazy kid things she hadn't been able to do because, well, chemo was completely draining and made her miserable. Her poor parents had wanted to treat her like china and tuck her away in a display cabinet somewhere. They'd loved her enough to learn to let go of that and recognize their worries might be unreasonable. Yet, she'd spent most of her childhood knowing they worried, so she'd hewed to a careful line in her life—one where she tried to not rattle their nerves too much, yet tried to find her own way at the same time.

Until her engagement blew up and she had to face the fact she'd never have children, at least not biologically, she'd played life safe. After that, she tossed caution aside and decided to follow her other dreams. She'd always dreamed about moving clear across the country, so she had. She couldn't say exactly when the kernel of that dream formed, but she remembered hours and hours of reading nature books and looking through wildlife magazines when she was in the hospital getting chemo. The world in those pictures seemed so far from the sterile hospital where she'd felt trapped. Learning she was infertile and getting dumped had jumpstarted her inside. Reeling and devastated, she'd set out to find happiness another way and immediately started planning to move. She'd landed in Diamond Creek and hadn't looked back yet. Her parents had mellowed with their worrying over the years, likely because she was still alive and breathing, and had sent her off with good wishes and visited plenty. Her mind circled back to Sawyer's question.

She looked to her side and realized he was still patiently waiting. She liked that about him. He wasn't antsy for conversation to move along at a fast clip. With the cluster of people waiting to be seated, he'd somehow managed to create a bubble of space by his mere presence. He definitely had that whole sexy military vibe going with just enough of an intimidation factor to make people step back and give him room. Well, that worked for her. She caught his eyes. "About the door...I don't mind. I was just curious."

He grinned, a slow, dangerous grin that sent flutters twirling in her belly and a hitch in her breath. Her body had a mind of its own when it came to Sawyer. She'd have to keep ahold of her sanity, but she was up for the challenge. "Good then. Would hate to argue about doors," he deadpanned.

Violet realized she needed to stay on her game. She'd lost her footing for a bit there, what with actually being interested in a man, but she wasn't about to let him get the upper hand. "If I had a problem with it, there would be no arguing," she countered.

At his chuckle, she glanced around, circling back to him. "See, it's a restaurant," she said, gesturing with her hand.

The inside of the plane hangar was expansive and instead of housing the small planes that flew all over Alaska, it contained a restaurant and brewery. The back end of the building housed the brewery behind a brick wall that separated it from the restaurant. The wide space above was decorated with model planes hanging from the ceiling, offering a whimsical touch to the space. While the side of the hangar where the entrance was had been left as is with a single door, the far side had replaced the massive garage doors with windows, offering a view of an adjacent field, which often had moose browsing in it and the mountains in the distance. Booths lining the walls and tables scattered in the middle easily filled the large space. Bright wall hangings and colorful rugs softened the noise in the cavernous space. As with most evenings, the restaurant was at capacity. Violet doubted there was ever a summer evening when the restaurant wasn't bustling.

Sawyer scanned the area, his perceptive gaze landing back on her. "So it is. Hard to tell from the outside. Gage swears this place is his second favorite after the lodge."

"The lodge restaurant is hard to beat, but

this place is good. Trust me, I grew up in New York City. I know good food when I find it."

"Ah, yes. You're a New Yorker. Alaska's a serious change of pace."

"And just what I needed."

He started to say something else when the hostess stopped beside them. "We have a booth for two in the corner. Every other party waiting is larger. Are you two ready?"

"Absolutely!" Violet said quickly.

Violet started to follow the hostess and almost stumbled when she felt Sawyer's palm land on her low back, the heat sifting through the fabric of her shirt. She'd started to convince herself all she'd needed was a little more time in Sawyer's company and his effect on her would wane. Nope. A subtle touch, and she was right back to butterflies and breathy with her pulse running off wildly.

CHAPTER 5

Sawyer looked across the table and wondered if he could find a way to finagle his way into Violet's bed before he had surgery. Her dark hair fell around her shoulders, gleaming under the lights, and the deep blue of her eyes drew him in every time she looked his way. Dinner with her had been more fun than he could remember having in, well, too damn long. He had fun with his family, but it was a different kind of fun. With Violet, everything felt sharp, clear and alive. Her forthright humor, sly sarcasm, and the warmth he sensed underneath drew him to her like a magnet.

They'd just had a good natured debate on baseball with Violet vehemently declaring baseball to be the most boring sport ever. She'd corrected herself and said golf was so bad it didn't really count as a sport in her mind. Sparring with her over silly topics was funny and served to notch up the desire thrumming in his veins.

He recalled his mother gently pointing out he'd become more serious over the last few years. He loved his career as a Navy SEAL—he thrived off the discipline and deeply respected the underlying mission of being a SEAL. Yet, he'd never deny it wasn't a sobering life. He and his team went on high-risk missions and often saw things he wished he could forget. His last mission had ended with him writhing in pain and being rushed off in a helicopter. He counted himself lucky to be alive, but it didn't change the fact he'd rather not see his career end like that. The last few months had been hard in more ways than one. Violet somehow nudged him out of that dark place inside.

Their waiter paused by the table, a lanky young man who was probably swimming in tips in this summer job. "Anything else guys?"

Violet cast her warm smile on the waiter. "Dessert. Tell me the options. Wait…" She paused and looked over at Sawyer. "Are you up for dessert?"

He was up for anything with her, but he was also always up for dessert. "Definitely," he said, winking before he'd realized it.

Her cheeks flushed slightly, her gorgeous eyes lingering on him for a moment, before she glanced back up at the waiter. "So tell me what's for dessert. Oh, and after dinner drinks. I need one of those too."

Sawyer had no idea what the waiter said, but when Violet asked him if he'd split something chocolate, he nodded. He could watch her all day. She was lively and amusing with everyone and had the waiter laughing when she bet him Sawyer wouldn't get an after dinner drink and would stick with beer.

Just to be let the waiter win, Sawyer ordered the same coffee with Kahlua she did. As the waiter turned away he called out. "Add a beer to that."

A balled up napkin bounced off of his shoulder. He glanced back to her to see her eyes snapping and her cheeks flushed. "Not fair! You're not even going to drink the coffee and Kahlua."

Heat went straight to his groin. He wanted to yank her across the table into his lap. Not the time and place for that though, so he shrugged. "Maybe I will. The beer's my back up."

She rolled her eyes and leaned back, brushing her hair off her shoulders. "Oh, fine."

"Hey, I just wanted the guy to win the bet with you. This way he'll get his five dollars plus our tip."

Her eyes widened and then she laughed. "Oh that's perfect! I wouldn't have held him to the bet. I was just teasing."

"Good to know."

Violet was quiet for a moment. She idly fiddled with the tie on her blouse, a tie that had been ridiculously tempting for him all evening. He wanted to rip it open and tear her shirt off. Her generous breasts curved up over the top, but he wanted to see more. She was just plain delectable.

The last few months he'd been so out of sorts he hadn't even considered dating, much less sex. She made him forget all of that and put everything in perspective. All he had to deal with was a cranky knee and a little shrapnel. He could do that if he had more of Violet to keep his attention elsewhere.

A short while later, they were walking out into the cool evening. Sawyer had quickly discovered evenings in Alaska seemed almost endless. Dusk lasted for hours with the sun starting its descent in late evening and light lingering until close to midnight. At the moment, the sky above the mountains was streaked with pink and purple, fading into the soft darkness. A half moon was rising above the bay in the distance. A raven called nearby, the distinct sound of its wings swishing through the air following its call.

His hand naturally landed on Violet's back, just where it dipped at her waist. The temptation to let his palm slide over the curve of her lush bottom was almost too much, but he managed. They walked in silence to his truck. He reached for the door right as she turned to glance up. The second her gaze caught his, a jolt of lust shot straight through him.

Her lips were right there, inches away. The air felt charged, the electricity between them humming to life. He waited a moment, forcing himself to give her the chance to turn away. She didn't. He could see the rapid beat of her pulse in her neck, her breath coming in short pants, mimicking his own. On the heels of the only deep breath he could manage, he closed the distance between them and fit his mouth over hers.

Oh damn. Kissing her was better than he

remembered. Her lips were plush and warm. She turned more fully to him with a sigh. He swept his tongue inside her mouth and stepped closer, one hand resting on the truck door behind her and the other threading into her silky hair. She drove him just as mad as she had last time he'd kissed her. Once their mouths met, she threw herself into it—her tongue tangled with his and she flexed against him. Holy hell, she felt so damn good—all lush curves against his hardness. He couldn't get enough and kissed her as if his life depended on it. Soft sounds came from her throat, driving him wilder inside. By the time he broke free to gulp in air, he had pressed her into his truck, every inch of her plastered against him. His cock was so hard, he was on the verge of exploding. He let his head fall into the sweet curve of her neck, breathing her in—she carried the subtle scent of vanilla with something tart mixed in.

Her breasts rose and fell with her breath, and he could've stayed right there for hours, savoring the feel of her. For the first time in months, he felt like himself again—his body nearly vibrating with the force of his desire for her. An odd side effect was a sense of strength and aliveness he hadn't felt since his injury. As they stood there, sounds eventually filtered into his awareness, and it occurred to him they were in a parking lot in public view. Oh sure, where they happened to be standing they were shielded from the main entrance to the restaurant, but it wasn't exactly private. He didn't give a damn, but wondered if perhaps Violet did.

He reluctantly lifted his head. She'd leaned her head back against the truck and opened her eyes slowly when he looked to her. In the smudgy light of dusk, he could still see the deep blue of her gaze, which was darker than usual. The air around them felt weighted with their desire. He stayed quiet, as she did as well. For several beats, they simply stared at each other. She swallowed and gave her head a little shake when a raven's call broke through the silence.

She licked her lips, and blood shot to his groin again. He was plenty aroused already, but damn she needed to stop that if he was going to keep a grip here.

"I suppose we should go," she finally said, her words husky.

He stared back at her, scrambling for purchase in his mind. He might not have been too focused on women since his injury and not had a life that allowed much room for them before that, but he'd certainly been more suave than this. He tried to recall if he'd ever been so muddled and caught by the whims of his body and was pretty damn certain he hadn't. He didn't want to move because that meant this moment would end—this moment with Violet soft against him, her lips swollen from their kiss and her cheeks rosy.

He was winging it, but he wasn't letting go that easy. He took a breath and steeled himself. "Probably, but I'd be lying if I said I wanted to have tonight end here."

Her breath drew in sharply, and her eyes widened. His body reacted on its own, his hips flexing just enough to feel the heat of her against his rock-hard cock. She bit her lip, a soft sound escaping and then pinned him with those sexy-as-hell eyes, sharp and snappy now.

"Not fair," she muttered.

He shrugged. "You existing isn't really fair, at least not as far as my body's concerned."

She laughed, her head falling back, tempting him to taste her neck. So he leaned forward and nipped, grinning in satisfaction at the goose bumps that rose on her skin.

"That's definitely not fair," she said, lifting her head again, her silky hair falling around her shoulders.

She didn't move and lifted a hand to trace along his collarbone. Damn if that single point of contact didn't send a jolt of electricity through him. "Okay then. Drive me home." She held his gaze for a long moment, the air taut around them. "You can walk me in."

He didn't know with certainty what that meant, but he'd take every moment she offered. With alacrity, he stepped back and ushered her into the car.

VIOLET WAS FAIRLY certain she might melt into a puddle in Sawyer's truck. That's how hot and bothered she was. She supposed she could count herself lucky the truck had been conveniently right behind her when Sawyer kissed her. Otherwise, she'd have fallen at his feet, awash in sensation. The space inside his truck felt electric. Meanwhile, she wondered just what the hell she'd gotten herself into. In the midst of her earlier obsessions about whether to call off this dinner date altogether, it had occurred to her Sawyer was only here temporarily. As far as her sources of gossip knew, he'd come to stay with his family while he recuperated. Those same sources of gossip also presumed he'd be returning to duty as a Navy SEAL once he was fully recovered. Violet didn't know what the situation really was, but all signs pointed to the fact Sawyer wouldn't be around too long. That tidbit had spun her in circles in her brain. Because her firm commitment to staying independent and not running the risk of falling for someone who wanted a family wasn't threatened if she happened to have a fling with someone who wouldn't be around long-term.

Her body was all kinds of happy about that because sweet hell did she want Sawyer. Something fierce. Her conscience was relieved as well because then she didn't have to worry about front-loading something casual with the announcement she didn't intend to let things get serious. She could avoid the natural questions about that. Talk about putting a damper on things. When she'd stared down her infertility, she'd thought she could date here and there and have a little fun as long as everyone knew where she stood. When most of her friends were complaining they couldn't find a guy who wanted to settle down, Violet promptly discovered that telling someone you couldn't have children was like dumping ice water all over them. She never even got to find out what might've happened because that was the fastest way to turn a little flirting into nothing.

She'd tried telling herself love and commitment weren't inextricably linked to having children, yet the intellectual knowledge couldn't seem to get past the emotional wall inside. Perhaps her emotions were tangled up in the way Ted dumped her, so abruptly on the heels of learning about her infertility, but the why and how didn't change her conundrum. She preferred not to let her heart meander accidentally in the wrong direction again. Sawyer's temporary stay here alleviated the burden of those worries for now.

She glanced up and realized they were at her apartment. Sawyer turned the truck into the parking area to the side of the building where a set of stairs led up to the small deck outside of her apartment. He turned the engine off, and they sat there, the air heavy around them. She was almost afraid to look at Sawyer. She was so flustered from their kiss and so turned on, she feared she'd tackle him. He saved her by opening the driver's side door.

Out of habit, she started to open her own, only to have Sawyer reach her door just as she fumbled for the handle. He winked when he swung it open. "Beat you to it," he said with a slow grin.

She swallowed and pointlessly tried to slow her rocketing pulse. She managed to climb out without falling on her face, although her knees were weak. Annoyed with herself for being so ridiculously affected by Sawyer, she turned to face him once he closed the truck door behind her. She opened her mouth to say god knows what, and he smoothly leaned forward and fit his mouth over hers. The intense need coiled tightly inside snapped loose. Her purse fell to the ground as she curled her hand around his neck and tugged him to her. There was nothing tentative about his kisses, it was as if the moment he acted, it became definitive. He swept his tongue in her mouth boldly and drew back to trace her lips and nip at them before diving in again.

Fire spread through her veins, and she stopped fighting her own battle against allowing herself to explore the madness. A distant siren rang inside. She simply couldn't say no, more to herself than to Sawyer. She wouldn't let it go too far. She'd just let herself have a little more than a few kisses. She tore her lips free with a gasp and grabbed his hand, pulling him behind her. She was half out of her mind with need, but she managed to recall he was dealing with a bum leg, so she didn't run, although she moved as fast as she possibly could and still call it slow.

She almost dropped her keys trying to open her door and then they stumbled through. The door clicked shut behind Sawyer. She dropped her purse and jacket to the floor and walked straight across the room to flick on a lamp in the corner. She turned to find Sawyer right behind her. Holy hell. He was all dark and strong, so damn sexy he took her breath away. She knew with certainty he left women swooning everywhere he went. Simply by existing with that dark hair, those steel gray eyes, and a body carved from stone, he was beyond delicious. Throw in the whole strong, sexy, military vibe where you just knew he'd save you if you needed saving, well that was more than swoon-worthy, it was panty-melting.

Her control, which she'd been keeping a firm grip on for years now, was frayed. Her breath came in shallow pants as he advanced on her. He stopped a hairsbreadth away from her, his eyes tracking over her. Streaks of heat raced through her, and her channel throbbed. He lifted a hand and tugged on the bow holding her shirt together. With the slightest pull, it came undone. Her belly clenched and she could barely catch her breath as he traced along the edge of the curved neck of her shirt. In two slow sweeps, it fell open. Her breasts felt heavy and taut, aching for his touch.

He dragged his finger across the sheer black silk of her bra, tracing a circle around one of her nipples, tight and begging for more. After he teased her mercilessly by doing the same to the other, he leaned forward and swiftly sucked her nipple into his mouth. She cried out, a jolt of hot pleasure scoring her. He stepped closer, and she thanked the stars she happened to be standing beside the back of the couch. Her hips bumped against it, but she didn't collapse. He set to drive her simply mad, drenching the silk of her bra as he toyed with her nipples. By the time he flicked his thumb under the clasp in the center, low moans were breaking from her throat and she was so close to a climax, it stunned her. Her channel was drenched and throbbing, slick with her need. The air whispered over her damp skin when her bra fell open, her nipples tightening further in response.

Sawyer lifted his head, his eyes locking with hers, his gaze dark. He was quiet, yet the intensity of his gaze sent a wash of heat through her. Without a word, he stepped back. For a flash, she felt bereft. Nothing more than a few inches between them, and she instantly wanted him right back where he'd been. Before she could form a thought, his lips closed over a nipple again, and she cried out. In seconds, he'd swiftly unbuttoned her jeans and slipped his hand inside, cupping her mound. Her hips were already rolling into his touch as he dragged his fingers back and forth over the silk between her thighs.

He bit down softly on one of her nipples, and she cried out. Restless, her hands roamed over his chest and she sighed when she dragged a hand down over the hard ridge of his arousal. With a muttered swear, he lifted his head and stepped between her thighs, bringing his mouth against hers in a scalding kiss. Just as his tongue swept into her mouth, he shoved the silk out of the way and drove two fingers into her channel. She came instantly, pleasure tightening and then snapping inside, spiraling through her in sharp shocks as her channel convulsed around his fingers.

He slowed his kiss and lifted his head. She was practically stunned, awash in pleasure and the pure release she felt. He slowly dragged his hand out and buttoned her jeans again. He started to put her bra back together when she realized he thought that was it. Oh no. She had to have more. Her need jolted her, and she pushed him back, roughly tearing his jeans open.

"No, you don't…" he started to say.

"I don't what?" she asked, cutting him off.

"Need to do that," he finished, his eyes scanning her face.

"It's not about need," she snapped, annoyed, but she couldn't say why. She wasn't about to let him come in here and leave her nearly boneless without making sure he felt the same before she was done.

He started to say something else, but groaned instead when she slid her hand over his briefs, curling her palm around his cock. She pushed his briefs out of the way and almost moaned when she saw his cock. Of course he'd have a gorgeous cock and of course, he was well-endowed. Nature had been beyond kind to Sawyer. It was like all of him, every inch just delectable. His skin was hot and velvety, and he groaned again when she leaned forward and dragged her tongue along each side of his cock. She didn't wait to take it slow. That was for another time. She took him into her mouth, savoring the subtle salty flavor. If he meant to stop her, he didn't try very hard. He mumbled her name once more and then one hand landed on the curve of her waist and the other gripped her hair. She held him lightly in her fist as she drew her mouth up and down the length of him.

With a guttural cry, he came in a rush. After he started to relax, she slowly pulled back, wiping her sleeve across her mouth as she stood. When she got a look at his face, she couldn't help but grin. He looked as stunned as she'd felt moments ago. She liked to be in control, so if she was going to lose it, it was only fair if she could turn the tables.

She rested her hips on the back of the couch and put her clothes back together. After a moment, he turned and propped beside her, a low laugh escaping. "Well then. I, uh, guess I didn't expect that."

She glanced sideways and saw he'd pulled his briefs and jeans back in place. His eyes scanned her face, and she suddenly felt vulnerable. She didn't know what he wanted. She reminded herself sternly that he was just here for a visit. She didn't need to worry about what he wanted. Before she realized what she was doing, she was talking, stumbling over herself to get out ahead of this.

"Well, that was fun. If you're worried I have expectations, no need. I know you're here temporarily, so nothing to worry about there," she said. Hearing her own voice, the forced brightness made her want to cringe.

Sawyer looked puzzled and almost hurt. She had to be imagining that. His eyes scanned her face. That tiny flash of hurt she thought she saw burrowed in her mind, a kernel of uncertainty forming. Her words had sounded so casual, as if she did this kind of thing easily. She didn't. Her heart was greedy and wanted more, but her dream of love and children had already been shattered spectacularly. She couldn't let herself think that glimmer in Sawyer's eyes meant anything because then she'd start wanting things she couldn't have.

"I can't say I had any expectations, but you make it sound like I'm just out for a little fun. Maybe I was once upon a time, and hell if I know what I expected, but I almost died a few months ago, so my perspective's a little different. You don't have to worry about expectations, but don't assume I'm just some guy looking for a little fun. I don't know what *this*..." He paused and gestured between them. "...is, but I know it's more than that."

Her heart gave a hard kick, and her breath

came out in a whoosh. Startled, her thoughts began spinning wildly, and she frantically reeled herself in. She stared back at him as he slowly straightened and faced her. He dipped his head and dropped a kiss on the side of her neck, sending a hot shiver through her. "Good night, Violet."

She was stuck where she was, incapable of moving it seemed, when he stopped by the door and looked back at her. "I'd like to see you again. My surgery's in four days. How about dinner or something else the day after tomorrow?"

She nodded swiftly. She might not be able to talk, but her body knew what she wanted even if her mind was spinning in circles.

He winked. "K. I'll text you."

A while later, she lay in bed, her mind replaying the evening again and again.

CHAPTER 6

"Hand me that hammer," Sawyer said, holding his hand out blindly from where he stood under the deck.

He was helping Gage replace a partially rotted beam under the deck behind the ski lodge. The back end of the lodge had a sprawling deck that stretched across the entire central portion of the resort. It was level with the second floor where the restaurant was, affording Sawyer the ability to be able to stand under the deck while he and Gage worked. He wiggled his fingers when the hammer wasn't forthcoming. "Any minute now."

He felt the rubber handle land in his palm and curled it in his grip. Leaning back, he glanced up at the section they needed to replace. They'd already put up supports on both sides of the beam. He set to work, prying the rusty nails out. He talked while he worked, knowing that while he couldn't see Gage, he was close by. "Dude, pretty sure this beam hasn't been touched since they built this place."

Gage's voice startled him because it was closer than he expected. He glanced over to find Gage dipping his head and stepping under the deck. "How bad is it?" Gage asked, stopping beside him.

Sawyer dropped another rusty nail in a bucket nearby. "Nothing you didn't already know. It's rotten," he said with a shrug, gesturing toward the beam with the hammer.

Gage rolled his eyes. "Thanks bro. I was curious if you can tell if it runs further than we thought."

"Doesn't look like it," Sawyer replied as he reached up and knocked loose some of the rotted wood. Inside of a few more minutes, he'd loosened the beam enough for Gage to use a reciprocating saw to remove the entire section.

They had a replacement section ready. Working together, they put it in place. With both of them Navy SEAL's, they shared an exacting approach to everything. Sawyer glanced to Gage after they'd removed the temporary supports under the deck and grinned. "Much better. What's your next project?"

Gage flashed a quick grin in return. "I'd like to replace all of the decking with composite so we don't have to worry about refinishing the damn thing every summer. In case you didn't notice, we've got a big deck."

Sawyer chuckled. "That you do."

"Not me. We," Gage said firmly.

Though Gage had been the one to move to Diamond Creek and renovate Last Frontier Lodge, largely on his own, he was insistent it was a shared endeavor among his siblings. Technically, although they had all inherited the lodge and its massive property when their grandmother passed away a few years ago, it was hard for Sawyer to feel like he was a part of it. He'd been overseas most of the time since Gage had moved up here. In what felt like nothing more than a blink of time, Garrett had followed Gage here and most recently Jessa. Becca was the only one of Sawyer's siblings *not* living in Diamond Creek, although she visited several times a year.

Sawyer's mind spun back to wondering what he might decide to do after his surgery. He supposed it came down to whether he wanted to be chained to an admin job in the military. His initial reaction to that was hell no. Even with bits of shrapnel annoying him and his knee making him gimpy, he was in close to peak condition. Yet, his leg wouldn't ever be one hundred percent again, which meant he wouldn't be in the condition necessitated for active duty as a Navy SEAL. He needed to make up his mind before it got made for him. Gage had reminded him too many times to count he'd be happy to have him stay and help him with the lodge. When Sawyer tried to argue he didn't want to take advantage, Gage had rolled his eyes and slapped a copy of Gram's will on his desk, pointedly reminded Sawyer he had a stake in the lodge as well.

With his mind chewing on those thoughts, Sawyer climbed the stairs onto the deck, noticing Gage had slowed his pace. He didn't like to be annoyed about that, but he was. "No need to wait for me, I'm only a few steps behind."

Gage glanced to his side, his eyes narrowing. "No need to be so cranky."

They cleared the last step onto the deck, and Sawyer mentally grimaced. "Sorry bro. That bad?"

They sat down in unison at one of the

picnic tables scattered about the deck. Gage ran a hand through his hair, his gray eyes landing on Sawyer. "Eh, not too bad. You were in a much better mood after you went out the other night though," he said with a sly grin.

Sawyer threw his head back with a laugh. He had most definitely been in a good mood after his dinner with Violet. Truth be told, Violet had been crowding his thoughts ever since. He caught Gage's gaze as his laugh slowed and he shrugged. "I suppose I was."

"Thought you said now wasn't a good time for a relationship."

Sawyer sobered and rolled his head from side to side, easing the subtle tension in his neck. "Still isn't," he finally replied.

Gage had this tendency to watch and wait, which sometimes drove Sawyer batshit crazy. For example, right now he didn't respond and simply kept his gaze on Sawyer. Sawyer shifted his shoulders, Violet strolling through his thoughts again. They'd had one date. That's it. He didn't think one date counted as anything close to a relationship, in fact he was damn confident it didn't. Yet, Violet had left a mark on him, and not just because the chemistry between them was hot enough to singe him.

He met Gage's gaze head on. "What's that look for?"

Gage arched a brow. "Seems like you had more to say."

Sawyer hooked his elbows on the edge of the table and leaned back, straightening his sore leg. "I dunno. Not sure what the hell I was thinking, but when I ran into Violet on my way out to go fishing, I asked her out to dinner. That's it."

Gage was quiet for another few beats before the slightest grin curved his mouth. "Huh? Well, sure seems like you like her."

Sawyer pondered whether *like* included thinking about when he'd see Violet again and replaying what it felt like when her channel clenched around his fingers. Oh, it had been beyond amazing when she gave him the blowjob of a lifetime, but it had been even better to watch her come apart. He also wondered if *like* meant wondering all kinds of things about her, such as how come she moved all the way across the country by herself, what her favorite food was, and what she looked like when she was asleep. Yeah, he liked her. He was many things, but coward wasn't one of them, so he caught Gage's eyes and smiled ruefully. "Yeah, I like her. Doesn't change the fact I'm about to go in for surgery in a few days."

Gage shrugged. "So what? You're alive and healthier than most. Before you know it, you'll be back to top form. If you like Violet, don't miss out on something good."

A screeching sound drew Sawyer's attention, and he glanced toward the ski slope directly behind them. This time of year, it was a grassy slope. "What's that?" he asked, just as a pair of magpies came hurtling out of the trees chattering like mad.

Gage chuckled. "That screech was an eagle. I'm guessing those magpies got a little too close for comfort."

Gage pointed to the side of the ski slope where towering spruce trees lined the slope. "There's an eagle perched right there. Great spot to hunt. He doesn't take well to being crowded."

As Gage spoke, the magpies flew high above the trees and made a dive toward the eagle who didn't move and let out another screech. Sawyer shook his head wonderingly. The eagle dwarfed the magpies, but they were a fearless bird and kept up their chatter as they flew across the slope into the trees on the other side. "Damn, it's like a nature channel here."

Gage nodded. "Pretty much. Anyway, eagles aside, if you ask me, you should take Violet out again."

"Already asked her," Sawyer countered with a laugh. He couldn't quite believe himself, but he had. He'd barely been able to think about anything other than her when he'd departed her place the other evening. All he'd known was he wanted to see her again.

Gage burst out laughing this time. When he caught his breath, he looked to Sawyer and shook his head. "Might as well stop acting like you're not interested."

At that moment, Gage's wife stepped out through the door that led into a hallway behind the lodge kitchen. Marley Hamilton was plain gorgeous, nice as could be, and perfect for Gage. Sawyer couldn't have been happier for him. Her auburn hair was pulled back in a ponytail that swung with her steps. She paused at Gage's side and rested her hips on the edge of the picnic table. "Hey guys, how'd the beam repair go?" Her green eyes bounced between them.

Gage curled an arm around her hips and

glanced up. "All taken care of. What're you up to?"

"Updating our reservations webpage and making it so everything automatically goes from payment to the server here. That'll make it easier at reception, so they don't have to switch screens. I dropped Holly off at Mom's a little while ago," she said, referring to their two-year old daughter who happened to be Sawyer's adored first niece.

"When will she be back home? I was hoping to take her with me to stop by Jessa's studio this afternoon," Sawyer said.

"You can pick her up if you want. You're her new favorite uncle, so she'll love it. I needed a few hours that didn't involve constant interruptions. Let me know when you're leaving, and I'll call my mom."

Sawyer glanced at his watch. "Not for another hour."

Gage glanced from Sawyer to Marley with a sly grin. "Sawyer likes Violet."

Marley grinned, almost gleefully. "Oh perfect! You need to focus on something other than your surgery. I don't know Violet too well, but Ginger says she's awesome."

Ginger was Marley's best friend and was often around the lodge with her husband Cam running the ski instruction programs here. Sawyer knew Ginger well enough to surmise she knew everything there was to know about anyone in the vicinity of Diamond Creek. He ran a hand through his hair and glared at Gage. "Thanks, dude. You just have to go and turn it into gossip."

Gage was unrepentant and shrugged. "It's not gossip if it's family."

Marley angled her head to the side. "I won't gossip, and Ginger won't either. It's just that she's nosy as hell and somehow manages to get people to tell her everything. If there's anything to know about Violet, she probably knows it."

Sawyer who'd never considered trying to glean information about a woman in his life was seriously considering finding a way to ask Ginger about Violet. Marley saved him from himself. "Don't worry over it. I'll find out everything Ginger knows so you won't have to embarrass yourself," she offered with a wide grin.

He fought to keep from thanking her because then he'd look as ridiculous as he felt. Marley dropped a kiss on Gage's cheek and headed back into the kitchen, leaving them at the table with Gage's shoulders shaking from laughter, while Sawyer wondered how he'd ended up this curious about a woman.

* * *

VIOLET TYPED at rapid fire speed, zooming through the charting for her last appointment and entering data from results into patient charts. She'd had a typically busy day, starting off with a little boy who'd come in for a leukemia screening. It wasn't the first time she'd drawn blood for a child whose pediatrician wanted to screen for the very cancer she'd had as a little girl. It always made her heart squeeze. This little boy, Dustin, had reached in and grabbed her heart. He was sweet, curious and funny and the best sport ever. But wiggly as hell. She could do her damnedest to make blood draws cause as little pain as possible, but a wiggly little boy made her job difficult. Against those odds, she'd still managed to distract him enough to do her job. His presence brought old memories slamming to the fore. So many visits to the lab, so many visits to the doctor and hospital. She'd been on a first name basis with half the staff at her local hospital.

One look in his mother's eyes, and she remembered that same look on her parents' faces

—controlled worry. His mother had been trying so hard to be cheerful and keep her chin up, but Violet had known it wasn't easy. She'd wanted to say something and spout off statistics about how good the recovery rates for childhood leukemia were, but she hadn't. It wasn't helpful, or appropriate. She knew from Dustin's referral from Dr. Quinn that he was there for leukemia screening, but she wasn't his doctor and certainly didn't know his symptoms. Good recovery rates weren't one hundred percent, so she'd held her tongue and tried to imbue the entire appointment with cheer. It was quite easy with Dustin tending toward cheery and warm all on his own.

Violet clicked save and powered down her laptop. She spun in her chair, scanning her small room. She never knew what to call her space. It wasn't an office per se, nor was it an exam room. She supposed it was a lab room, but it was hers alone. That was one thing she loved here at the hospital in Diamond Creek. It was busy, but not like New York City hospitals were busy. She'd worked in two there, and it had been chaotic to say the least. In both places, she'd shared space with many others. Here, she had her own area, so she could keep it the way she liked. It was the usual cool and sterile because it needed to be. She'd added a dash of color to the room with a bright purple curtain over the window.

She stood to quickly put away a few things. She paused by the window to look outside. When she'd applied for the position here, it never occurred to her she'd have a view right from the hospital. She laughed to herself because it was harder to find a place that didn't have a view here than the opposite. Diamond Creek Hospital was situated slightly above the center of town on the hillside, offering a sweeping view of downtown and Kachemak Bay. It was early evening with the sun just now beginning to dip down the sky. She'd only experienced one summer in Alaska so far and was still getting used to the endless days. Her small window was almost smack in the middle of the hospital, offering a direct view of the bay and mountains on its far side. Boats dotted the water, and the light was soft, almost ethereal.

She lingered over the view before getting ready to leave. In between appointments, Sawyer kept interrupting her train of thought. Well, it was the opposite rather. The rest of her life kept interrupting her thoughts, which seemed stuck on Sawyer. She spent half of her time replaying what it felt like to have him blow her mind and leave her nearly in a puddle the other evening. The other half the time she wondered just what the hell she'd been thinking. She was in deep infatuation with him after only one dinner date. She'd thought herself long past this tendency. In her early twenties—she felt ancient at twenty-nine now—she'd wanted nothing more than to be swept off her feet. Back then, she fancied herself in love time and again. After she'd gotten over the demise of her engagement to Ted, she'd taken a clear look back and deduced she didn't really know if she and Ted had been well suited. She'd wanted to be in love, and he went along with it. It was hard to believe he actually loved her. If he had, it was hard to imagine he could've so easily walked away.

Violet gave her head a shake. She didn't need to dwell on the past. She needed to stay clear-eyed about her future and not fall head over heels in love. Sawyer made her feel silly and goofy. She used to love this part of dating —the fun rush of infatuation and wondering where things might go. She'd learned the hard way that this fun part didn't mean the fantasy ending would come true. Sawyer was all kinds of amazing—sexy as hell with body honed from his years in the military, funny, nice, and clearly a family oriented guy. All through dinner, comments about his siblings and parents popped up. She couldn't imagine he didn't eventually want everything else that went with family. Therein lay the crux of her problem. She couldn't let herself fall for someone like that because she'd be setting herself up for another fall, and it wasn't really fair to him either.

Every time she brushed up against the train of thought, anxiety knotted in her chest, so she shoved the thoughts away. Nothing to be done. She couldn't change the fact she was infertile. She needed to stop being all warm and fuzzy inside—okay, warm and fuzzy didn't cut it, more like burning up with need.

She stepped outside and walked quickly across the parking lot to her car. She'd been trying to figure out how to graciously bow out of another dinner with Sawyer. He'd surprised her by asking, and she'd surprised herself by saying yes. She didn't like to think she was a coward, but right about now, she was thinking she'd rather text him and cancel. It wasn't that she didn't want to see him. It was the opposite. She wanted to see him way too much, and the little problem she'd thought herself long over, the one where she dove into infatuation, had come back with a vengeance. It didn't help one bit that Sawyer was so worthy of infatuation. He was like a walking advertisement for tall, dark and dangerous, the kind of dangerous where you just knew he'd save you at the slightest hint of danger. To make it even worse, he was nice and funny. With a sigh, she climbed into her little hatchback and headed into town.

iolet wheeled her grocery cart around the end of an aisle, coming to an abrupt stop when she bumped into someone. "Oh! I'm so sorry!" she exclaimed, her hand flying to her chest when she glanced up and saw she'd just collided with Ginger Nash, an acquaintance on the way to being a friend.

Ginger turned and rested her elbow on the handle of her grocery cart. She was grinning, which at least told Violet she hadn't bumped her too hard.

"Are you okay?" Violet asked with an apologetic smile.

Ginger nodded, her shiny dark hair swinging around her shoulders as she did. "Oh yeah. I've got plenty of padding on these hips," she said with a roll of her eyes.

Ginger was by no means overweight, but she also wasn't stick thin, which Violet appreciated, seeing as she was on the curvy side herself. "Padding's a good thing. Keeps me warm," Violet replied. "Anyway, sorry I almost ran you over."

She left unsaid that she'd decided to run a few errands and was distracted while she was trying to avoid calling Sawyer to cancel. She was tempted, oh so tempted, to just text him, but that rubbed her the wrong way. She faced things head on, and she would call him. Meanwhile, she had plenty of things to do to keep her busy, including a run through the grocery store. Her refrigerator was close to bare. She loved to cook, but with only herself to cook for, it was easy to rely on quick dinners.

Ginger shrugged. "No worries. How've you been?" she asked.

"You know, nothing new. Busy with work, life and what-not."

Violet considered her life briefly. She liked her life here in Diamond Creek. She had a job she loved, a cute little apartment, and a gorgeous area to explore. This was her second summer here, and she was working her way through the many possible outdoor activities. Last summer, she'd hiked just about every trail in the nearby vicinity. This summer, she'd focused on getting out on the water. She'd taken several kayaking trips and hoped to go fishing soon, along with taking a flight tour. She'd gradually started to get to know people in Diamond Creek. To be honest, the move had been so huge for her, she was only now settled in enough to feel like she was part of the community. She'd first met Ginger about six months ago when they both stopped to help an elderly woman who had a flat tire. Violet had been halfway under the woman's car when Ginger arrived. Her thoughts circled back. So yeah, life was busy and mostly good. Something about Sawyer made her want more.

"How about you?" she belatedly asked.

Ginger smiled again, this time slyly. "Can you tell?"

"Um, can I tell what?" Violet countered, mystified by Ginger's question.

Ginger looked down at her stomach and back up. Violet was still confused. "Um, I'm lost here."

Ginger sighed dramatically. "I'm pregnant! You probably can't tell because of all that padding we just discussed."

Violet couldn't help but laugh. Ginger was plain funny. When she managed to stop, she looked more closely at Ginger, noticing the slightest curve in her belly. "Congratulations! When's your due date?"

"Forever it seems, but it's really only six more months. Baby's due in January, and we've agreed to not find out whether it's a girl or boy. I told Cam I need something to surprise me after all that work. Well, that and the morning sickness."

Violet laughed at Ginger's burdened expression, if only because Ginger was laughing herself. Violet had spent a few months in therapy after she learned about her infertility and watched her fiancée walk away without a backward glance. For the most part, she'd made peace. Funny how you made peace with circumstances because you had no choice otherwise. She might've come to terms with the reality she had to face, yet she hated that it was impossible not to think for a second about what she couldn't have at moments like this. For a flash, she felt an overwhelming sense of loss and then it passed. She looked over at Ginger's twinkling blue eyes and took a deep breath.

"Still have morning sickness, huh?" Violet asked.

Ginger nodded emphatically. "Yes! Oh my God, it sucks. Dr. Marshall keeps telling me it should get better. But I'm officially past my first trimester, so I'm ready for it to end. Anyway, so that's my big news. Onto you. What's this I hear about you and Sawyer Hamilton?"

Violet's mouth fell open and her cheeks got hot instantly. How in the world Ginger knew she'd been on a date with Sawyer was beyond her. "What...how...?" she sputtered.

Ginger's sly grin was almost too much. "Okay, I know you've only known me a few months, but someone should've told you I usually find out everything about everyone."

Violet rested her elbows on her grocery cart and shook her head slowly. "How would I know that? I've only lived here like a year. People are really friendly, but it was pretty clear I had to prove I was sticking around before anyone started treating me like I was local. So, no. I didn't know you were gossip central," she said with a sigh.

Ginger's smile shifted from sly to warm. "Oh, don't be embarrassed. I'm not really gossip central. It's just I like to know things and people tend to tell me stuff. It helps that

I've lived here most of my life. The reason I knew about Sawyer wasn't actually gossip, although trust me it will be if he sticks around town. You've met Marley, right?" she asked.

Violet knew Marley was married to Gage Hamilton and another long-time Diamond Creek resident. She knew her more because her mother, Holly, was a nurse at the hospital. "Oh yeah. Her mom works with me, so I've seen her a few times when she stops by."

"Oh right. Anyway, Gage asked Marley to ask me to find out about you." Ginger paused, arching a brow, her grin returning to sly. "Because he thinks Sawyer really likes you."

Violet's mouth fell open, and her cheeks got a little hotter. Questions swirled through her mind. Rising through the swirl in neon: *Sawyer really likes you!* Meanwhile, all she could do was stare at Ginger.

Ginger's gaze shifted to curious. "Well, I guess the feeling's reciprocated then. You know, Sawyer's got that whole tall, dark and dangerous look down to a science. He's not my cup of tea, but no one's been since I met Cam, so it's not his fault." Her eyes narrowed. "Okay, you have an assignment."

Violet's mind was still spinning over Ginger's comment that Gage thought Sawyer really liked her. "An assignment?"

Ginger nodded firmly. "Gage is worried about Sawyer and wants him to stay. If he's into you, maybe he'll stay. That's your assignment. Make Sawyer stay in Diamond Creek."

Violet's mouth fell open for the second time inside of a few minutes. This time she snapped it shut. "Are you crazy?" she finally asked.

Ginger, whom Violet had previously considered sane, shook her head. "Don't think so." She looked completely serious, as if her request was perfectly normal.

Violet tried to make sense of this 'assignment' and finally just laughed. "Look, Sawyer and I had dinner. Once. I don't know what Gage thinks, but Sawyer and I don't really know each other all that well." Her mind flicked to the feel of his fingers buried inside her while she came. She batted that thought away. So, they had amazing chemistry. That didn't mean she needed to hop onto this absolutely crazy idea of Ginger's. That part of her that dove right into relationships, or used to, was all but dancing around. Sanity, she needed sanity.

"Ginger, I know you don't know me all that well yet…"

Ginger cut in. "Maybe, but I know you're awesome."

"Really?" Violet said with a laugh.

"Yeah. The first time I met you, your legs were sticking out from under Mrs. Stevens' car. It was almost zero out and there was snow everywhere. Only super nice people help cranky old women change tires and crawl under their car to find the keys they dropped on the ground."

"Oh yeah. I forgot about that," Violet replied with a shrug. "Anyway, back to your point. There's all kinds of reasons it's not a good idea for me to be in charge of convincing Sawyer to stay here, not the least of which is the fact one date doesn't mean a whole lot." As she tried to sound casual, her pulse accelerated and heat slid through her veins. She could tell herself all kinds of things, but those few mo- ments with Sawyer had just about melted her inside and out. It was one hell of a date, and she couldn't stop thinking about when she might see him again. Problem, this was a problem.

"Oh fine," Ginger said with an elaborate sigh. "How about you join me at Sally's for dinner with Marley and Delia instead?"

Violet experienced a moment's hesitation.

"Are you sure? I don't want to impose."

Ginger rolled her eyes. "Of course I'm sure! I've been meaning to ask you to get together, but you know how life is. I get busy and forget. You're standing in front of me now and I'm headed over to Sally's right after this. Come on, it'll be fun."

Violet smiled from the inside out. She'd been dipping her toes in the social world here, but it was slow going. "Okay. What time should I meet you there?"

"How about you follow me now?" Ginger asked.

* * *

SAWYER IDLY SPUN his keys on his index finger as he walked alongside Gage into Sally's, a local bar and restaurant. He'd been here a few times before when he was visiting. They were meeting Garrett for burgers and beer. The parking area was crowded even though it was still fairly early. They pushed through the dou-ble-swinging doors into the restaurant. The building had once been a barn and retained the feel of one. The inside was spacious with its high ceiling. The rough wood of the old barn had been finished to a gleam throughout. One side held the bar with small tables and a stage for music, while the other side held the restaurant. There was a cluster of people waiting in front, but Gage threaded his way through, glancing to Sawyer as he did. "Garrett texted that he snagged a booth already."

Garrett gave a wave from where he was seated on the far side of the restaurant, and they quickly made their way to him. Sawyer slid into the booth across from Garrett who grinned and winked. "Hey guys! Damn lucky I got here a few minutes ago. As soon as I sat down, a line showed up. Place is nuts this time of year."

"Is there anywhere that isn't this busy in the summer?" Sawyer asked.

Gage and Garrett glanced at each other and then him. "Nope," Gage said.

Sawyer glanced around. The crowd was a mix of tourists and locals. The tourists tended to stand out, mostly because they were usually burdened with shopping bags and cameras. Random wildlife sightings were so common in Alaska, it was best to have a camera handy at all times if you were visiting. Sally's had a warm, inviting feeling. Booths circled the room on the outer wall with a cluster of tables in the middle. The décor was simple with polished wood everywhere and basic white linens. He leaned back and took a breath, letting it out slowly. He could get used to more days like today. He enjoyed working on projects around the lodge and could see they were endless. He liked something to focus on, but the best part was being with his family. Gage was an easy brother to be around. Sawyer had looked up to him when they were growing up and followed him into the Navy and then into SEAL training. It was nice to be on the other side of that life and just relax with his brothers.

Garrett waved their waitress over who quickly took their drink order, left menus behind, and turned to the next table. Sawyer flipped the menu open and then glanced between Gage and Garrett. "Just tell me what's good."

"Salmon burger," Garrett said firmly.

"Ditto," Gage added.

"Okay, salmon burger it is," Sawyer said, promptly closing his menu and sliding it to the end of the booth.

"So what'd you guys do today?" Garrett asked as he folded the table napkin into a perfect paper airplane.

"Fixed that beam on the back deck and took care of some minor repairs. Any chance you can stop by this weekend to help us replace some of the decking?" Gage asked.

"You're doing that now?" Sawyer asked. Gage had mentioned this afternoon that he wanted to, but Sawyer hadn't realized he meant now.

Gage nodded and leaned back as their waitress arrived with their beers. "You guys ready to order?"

"Three salmon burgers and an order of artichoke crab dip," Garrett said.

The waitress grinned. "Easy enough. Anything else?" she asked, her eyes bouncing between Sawyer and Gage.

When they shook their heads in unison, she spun away. Sawyer glanced to Gage again. "So the decking?"

Gage shrugged. "Sure. After we finished up today, I looked up the price for the composite decking. It's on sale right now, so I ordered enough to replace all the decks. You know me. I like to get stuff done."

Garrett laughed and arched a brow. "I think it's a family trait. The getting things done, that is. As for this weekend, I can come up tomorrow. You hankering to get this done before gimpy's surgery," he said with a wink in Sawyer's direction.

"Seriously, dude? I'm not that gimpy. I'm happy to help with the deck. About all I can't do is run right now. Once they take care of my leg, give me a few weeks, and I'll beat you in a race," Sawyer said with a roll of his eyes.

Garrett winked again. "Course you will."

Conversation moved on to other matters with their food arriving somewhere along the way. While Gage and Garrett were discussed the merits of updating the legal setup for the lodge business, Sawyer leaned back and idly twirled his beer bottle between his fingers as he looked around the restaurant. Marley walked in, followed by Delia and Ginger. Just as Sawyer was about to ask Gage and Garrett if they'd planned to meet them here, Violet walked through the arched entrance into the restaurant section right behind them. Awareness sliced through him, and his eyes moved over her hungrily. To say he'd had a few too many replays of their heated encounter the other evening was an understatement. He'd been impatient for tomorrow to arrive so he could see her again, and here she was. Marley paused and looked around. The booths were all at capacity. After a moment, she said something to Ginger who snagged the waitress, while Marley walked over to where they were sitting.

"Okay guys. I know you're here for a little brother bonding, but we're here for girls' night and there's nowhere to sit. How about you let us join you?" Marley asked with her eyes locked on Gage.

Sawyer was well aware Gage pretty much couldn't say no to Marley for anything, so her question was rather pointless. He didn't mind a bit because it looked like Violet was with them, which meant he'd get some bonus time with her. "Fine with me," he said quickly.

Gage nodded. "Of course. There's not enough room for everyone though."

"Already thought of that. Ginger's checking to see if we can push a table up at the end," Marley replied. "Hang on." She turned away and met Ginger halfway across the restaurant.

Gage looked to Sawyer. "Well, that was quick," he said with a grin.

"Huh?"

"You jumped all over the chance to get crowded into a booth with Violet."

Garrett burst out laughing. Before Sawyer had a chance to reply, Marley was returning to their booth with Ginger, Delia and Violet on her heels.

CHAPTER 8

$\mathcal{V}$iolet thought she might melt on the spot, which would be mortifying to say the least. Somehow, what was supposed to be dinner with Ginger and her friends had turned into dinner with the Hamilton men, all three of them. Gage and Sawyer looked so alike it was startling, both drop dead sexy with their chocolate brown hair, steel gray eyes and bodies carved from stone and honed in the military. Garrett had a slightly more polished look and darker, sharper edges to him. Collectively, they epitomized dark and sexy. Funny thing was, Violet could objectively see those qualities in Gage and Garrett, yet there was no zing with them. It was more of a simple appreciation.

With Sawyer, there was serious zing. It wasn't just zing, it was hot, sizzling madness in her body was what it was. Somehow she'd ended up crowded between Sawyer and Ginger in the booth, which meant she could feel Sawyer's hard muscled thigh against hers. Who'd have thought she could get turned on by nothing more than the feel of a guy's leg? It was ridiculous. She was suffused with heat and got all hot and melty inside every time Sawyer locked eyes with her.

Somehow she was managing to follow along with conversation, although she was distracted beyond belief. Ginger elbowed her in the side. "What do you mean baseball is boring?" Ginger demanded, pinning Violet with her sharp gaze.

Violet had completely lost track of the conversation and had absolutely no idea why they were talking about baseball. "I'm sorry. You lost me. What about baseball?"

She heard a low chuckle from Sawyer, which sent a prickle up her spine. His hand slid onto her leg and gave a squeeze. She thought she might just die of mortification. Her panties were damp, and her pulse was all over the place. Dammit! She needed to focus, not act like a flaky idiot.

Ginger's eyes flicked from Violet to Sawyer and back again, a subtle gleam entering her gaze. Violet didn't dare look his way. Ginger cleared her throat. "Sawyer said you said baseball is boring," she said slowly. "Have you ever played baseball?"

Violet vaguely remembered that she'd complained about how boring it was to watch baseball the other night during dinner with Sawyer. Like now, she'd been so internally overwhelmed, she hadn't thought much of anything she said. Yet, she really did find baseball boring. She met Ginger's gaze and did her damnedest to ignore the feel of Sawyer's palm curled over her thigh. "Actually I haven't. Since I had leukemia when I was little, I couldn't play at first. After that, well, I love my parents to pieces, but they'd have wrapped me in bubble wrap if they could've. So no baseball for me. Watching it is a bit boring if you ask me."

Ginger nodded along, her eyes considering. "Okay, I'll admit watching it on TV is pretty slow, but now that I know you missed out on playing, you have to play. It's a little late this year, but our local league plays all the way into the fall. We take our good weather seriously. I help manage one of the teams, so you should play. We'll let you join late," she said with a firm nod as if it had already been decided.

Before Violet had a chance to respond, Sawyer spoke up. "How many teams are in the local league here?"

Ginger arched a brow and lifted her chin. "Three. We play each other and sometimes go to Kenai and Homer. Don't make fun just because Diamond Creek is small. We know how to have a good time and kick ass while we're at it."

Violet glanced in Sawyer's direction when he chuckled. Serious mistake. Her eyes collided with his, her belly somersaulted, and raw need jolted her. She looked away so fast, she was surprised she didn't get whiplash.

"Wasn't making fun. Just curious. You guys play?" Sawyer asked, looking to his brothers. If he was as rattled as she was, it sure didn't show. He managed to carry on an actual conversation and look like a normal person while he was at it.

"Of course," Garrett said with a grin. "I think it's mandatory, right?" he asked, his teasing gaze flicking to Ginger.

Delia, who Violet had barely met, lightly punched him on the shoulder. "It's not mandatory and you know it. Although Nick would be devastated if we didn't play."

Violet was still trying to piece together all the social details of the group. She knew who went with who. In this case, Delia and Garrett were married and appeared blissfully happy. Yet, she had no idea who Nick was and suddenly worried if she should have some clue. "Not to sound stupid, but who's Nick?" she asked.

"Our son," Garrett said promptly. "He loves anything to do with throwing a ball, so we play every year."

"Got it. Is there anyone here who doesn't play?" Violet asked next.

Gage was chuckling, which led Ginger to throw a napkin at him. He caught it and neatly folded it before laying it on the table. "You know we all love it, but you are kinda bossy about it," he said with a wink.

"I think it's safe to say we're the only two people here who aren't playing. I'm definitely out for now until after my surgery, but you should play," Sawyer said. "I joined a few games last year when I was visiting, and it's fun as hell. No skills necessary."

Ginger smiled widely. "See! That's why you

should play," she said, looking expectantly at Violet.

Violet didn't care so much about baseball, but she did want to have more chances to get to know friends here, so she was game. "I'm in. Just tell me when and where. You'd better not give me grief for my lack of skills. I've never played."

Ginger slipped her arm over Violet's shoulders and gave a squeeze. "Perfect! Don't you worry. All skills levels are welcome."

"Including none?" Violet countered.

Ginger nodded emphatically before tugging on her jacket, which had slipped down behind her, and standing. "Okay, my work here is done. I need to get home. All you lovebirds are making me miss Cam." She caught Violet's gaze. "Next practice is Sunday at three. We play at the high school field. Just drive around back, and you can't miss it. See you then!" She waved and spun away.

The next few minutes were a jumble of everyone getting their things together and departing gradually. Before Violet realized what had happened, Garrett and Delia were walking toward the door, his hand slipped into the rear pocket of Delia's jeans, and Violet was alone in the booth with Sawyer.

She glanced to him, butterflies amassing in her belly and a hot shiver racing over her skin at the look in his eyes. She tried to catch her breath, but it didn't go so well. She swallowed and tried to gather her thoughts. "So, uh, I guess…"

Sawyer cut in decisively. "Don't go. Not yet."

Violet desperately didn't want to go. She was on fire inside and out and wanted to climb on Sawyer's lap and eat him up. This was a problem—a serious problem. Crazy, burning lust aside, the more time she spent with him, the more she liked him. The more it was also obvious family was central to him, something she couldn't give him. She stared at him, caught in his gaze. She was tempted, oh so tempted, to give into the thundering roar of desire she felt. Its intensity shocked and terrified her.

She tore her eyes free from his and stood up, so abruptly her knees bumped the table hard enough to send an empty beer bottle toppling over. It rolled off and hit the floor with a clatter, breaking into pieces and effectively snapping the moment of madness between them. Flushed inside and out, she glanced to Sawyer and away to find the noise had drawn the attention of neighboring customers. Perfect. She leaned over and started to reach for the broken bottle when Sawyer's voice cut in.

"Don't cut yourself," he said quickly.

She felt him sliding out of the booth seat behind her, and she quickly straightened. Right, picking up a broken bottle was not the wisest plan.

At that moment, their waitress arrived with a dustpan and broom. She swept up the mess and threw a warm smile in their direction when she glanced to the table and saw the generous tip. Between the group, they'd respectively left a healthy pile of cash on the table for her tip. "Thanks! You two have a good night," she said before turning and walking away to dispose of the broken glass.

Violet looked to Sawyer who was standing beside her. His eyes held a question in them, and she didn't care to ponder what it was. She grabbed her purse and jacket. "I have to go," she said. He was quiet and just stood there, one hand tucked in his jeans and oozing all kinds of sexy military man vibes. All he had to do was stand there and she melted inside. She couldn't give herself a chance to second-guess herself. She'd plain lost her mind the other night and couldn't let herself fall deeper into this infatuation with Sawyer. She forced herself to meet his gaze and tried to slow her thundering pulse. "I can't have dinner with you tomorrow," she blurted out and started to hurry away. Spinning back, her gaze landed on him again. She was so tempted to forget all of her reservations. Yet, she couldn't. "I hope your surgery goes well," she managed and then practically ran out of the restaurant.

SAWYER CONSIDERED FOLLOWING VIOLET. Hell, his body was in near revolt because he didn't. He'd spent the last few hours in a state of perpetual arousal. With her cozied up beside him in the booth, it had been all he could do to keep his hands mostly to himself. The restaurant door swung closed behind her, while he wrestled internally. No matter how much he wanted her, and damn did he want her, something about the look in her eyes kept him from racing after her. There was that and the fact he couldn't really 'race' after anyone right now. Perhaps in another month after his surgery he could. He gave himself a mental shake and slowly walked out.

Gage had left with Marley, so Sawyer was

on his own for the drive back to the lodge. He couldn't help but wonder what put that look in Violet's eyes. He wouldn't call it fear because that wasn't how it felt. Whatever it was, she was backing off and fast. For a guy who hadn't even considered a woman seriously for years, he didn't know what to think of his train of thought. Aside from the raw lust Violet evoked in him, she made him curious. He wanted to know everything about her, most especially what was driving her to push him away.

CHAPTER 9

"Seriously, Jess. You don't have to wait here the whole time," Sawyer said, glancing across the waiting room in the surgery clinic.

Jessa gave him a stern look, which was so unusual for her, he burst out laughing. She narrowed her eyes. "What's so funny?"

He glanced to Becca, his other sister and Garrett's twin. She narrowed her eyes as well. "We get to be worried about you. You're having surgery," Becca said, her blue gaze sweeping over him.

They were collectively waiting at the clinic in Anchorage for Sawyer to go in for his surgery. He hadn't known Becca was flying up to meet them until Jessa insisted on stopping by the airport. It was barely past six in the morning, and Becca had taken a red-eye flight from Seattle to meet them. She appeared more rested than he felt. Becca was so much like Garrett it tended to amuse the rest of them. They shared glossy dark hair and sharp blue eyes, along with both being brilliant, aggressive attorneys. While Garrett had once been the go-to corporate lawyer in Seattle, he now did legal work for just about everything in Southcentral Alaska. Becca applied her brilliance to being a prosecutor specializing in domestic violence cases. She was less of a softy on the outside than Jessa, but just as warmhearted underneath. He should've expected her to show for his surgery because that's the kind of sister she was.

He thanked the stars his brothers had enough sense to leave him be. If it were Gage or Garrett going in for surgery, he figured they'd feel hen-pecked enough by their sisters. He glanced from Becca and Jessa and ran a hand through his hair, leaning back in his chair. "Whatever. You can worry, but I'll be fine. All they need to do today is clean out the bits of shrapnel."

Becca nodded. "Right, but it's still surgery."

Sawyer was about to reply when a nurse

entered from the door to the side of the waiting room. He recognized her from when he'd met with her a month or so ago when he first arrived in Alaska. She walked across the room and sat down in a chair across from him. "Are you ready?" she asked with a warm smile. The nurse had a soft air about her. She was round all over with kind blue eyes and curly gray hair.

"Absolutely," he said with a nod as he stood. "I'd like to say I remember your name, but I'm afraid I don't."

"It's Martha. Who should I check with if there are any complications?" she asked, her eyes flicking from him to his sisters.

"Both of us," Jessa said firmly.

"We're his sisters, and he signed releases," Becca added.

Sawyer chuckled. Leave it to Becca to make sure the nurse knew that detail. She'd herded him to the check-in desk as soon as they arrived and insisted he sign releases so if anything went wrong they could speak with the doctors. He hadn't minded a bit, but it was so like Becca to take care of all the practical matters immediately.

Martha grinned. "Ah, I see he's in good hands with you two. Well, not to worry. We'll take good care of him." She glanced at her watch and from him to his sisters. "He'll go in for prep now and surgery is scheduled for eight. He should be out in roughly an hour. You can visit him in the recovery room once they clear him for visitors. Any questions before I take him away?"

Jessa stood and gave him a quick hug, while Becca grinned and gave a small wave. "We'll be right here. Love ya!"

At that, he followed Martha through the doorway and into a hallway. The clinic had done their best to add warm touches with photos of Alaskan scenery on the walls. Perhaps it was because he didn't enjoy being injured or the fact that he'd been dealing with the annoying pain in his leg for going on three months now and hated every minute of being physically limited. No matter the cause, every hospital and medical clinic felt cold and sterile. He was beyond ready for his surgery, just so he could finally ditch the pain and figure out what the hell he wanted to do next.

Martha was as warm and kind as her smile. Between her and the jovial anesthesiologist, he was soon relaxing on a wheeled bed as the sedative they gave him took hold. He'd been swatting away thoughts of Violet since the other evening when she cancelled their dinner and left in a rush. Yet, once he started to tumble into the woozy place created by the relaxing sedatives, she sauntered into his thoughts. He wanted to know all kinds of things about her, most specifically what was she afraid of? He didn't doubt the lightning hot chemistry between them, so he was pretty damn sure he hadn't misread that. He was a bit unsettled with the depth of his curiosity about her, but right now, he wasn't. He wished she were here, so he could ask her.

As he lay there, drifting in his thoughts, the curtain in front of the small cubicle where he was waiting rolled back. Martha stepped into the area, resting her hand on the edge of his narrow bed. "We're about ready for you. How are you feeling?"

"A little out of it, but that's not a bad thing," he replied.

She smiled. "Not at all. Any last questions before we take you into the operating room?"

He thought for a minute and then his mouth dumped out the only question he really had at the moment. "How do you know when someone's really special?"

This had been on his mind for days. Raw, sexual chemistry was one thing. He'd experienced that before. What he hadn't experienced was this curiosity about a woman, this pull to know what lay beyond the electric connection he felt with Violet.

Martha's eyes held his, a momentary look of confusion dissolving into kindness. "Ah, you're floating off and wondering about all kinds of things. You must've met someone special or you wouldn't even be asking."

"I wouldn't?"

Martha shook her head. "Nope. It's when you start wondering that you know." She gave his hip a pat. "Let's get you taken care of, and then you can get back to sweeping whoever she is off her feet."

"You sound pretty confident about that," he said, pondering in a drifty sort of way that he was usually confident about almost everything. Confidence was an absolute necessity as a Navy SEAL. He'd succeeded in his career by trusting his strength and skills in all situations. Yet, Violet rattled him in ways entirely unfamiliar to him.

Martha grinned. "Oh hon, you are definitely going to sweep her off her feet if you haven't already."

While Sawyer was hoping she was right, an orderly appeared and next thing he knew, he was being wheeled down the hallway and into a room with bright lights overhead.

* * *

"Mom, you can stop worrying any day now," Violet said, swallowing a sigh and walking to stand in front of her apartment windows.

She was on the phone with her mother who was worrying about her former fiancée's new wife posting all over social media about being pregnant. Of course, Violet had seen the posts. The wonderful world of social media was nice for keeping in touch, especially from a distance. However, it made it painfully hard to create clear boundaries when you wanted to separate yourself from an old relationship. She had a number of friends in New York in common with Ted. They'd dated for two years before getting engaged. She wasn't one to try to shun people and honestly was well over Ted. His abrupt dumping had been harsh, but it actually helped her move on. Coming to terms with her infertility had been more of a battle when all was said and done. She knew Ted wanted kids, so she could mostly find it in her to be happy for him. Yet at moments, it was like rubbing a bit of salt in the wound to see his new wife's baby bump popping up here and there when shared online by mutual friends.

However, having her mom bring it up was annoying. She'd spent much of her life telling her parents not to worry.

Her mother's sigh came through the phone. "You are so stubborn. I know you're fine. If I'm honest, I'm more annoyed about how he treated you, and I don't think he deserves to be happy," her mother said.

Violet could actually see her mother's mouth tighten in a line of disapproval and couldn't help but laugh. "Oh geez, Mom. Ted did what he did. I moved on. Whether he deserves to be happy or not isn't really something I worry about much these days."

"Oh fine. You're a better person than me sometimes. Anyway, how are you? Your dad and I want to come out for another visit soon. Does it matter when we come?"

As usual, her mother threw more than one question at her. Violet focused on the first one. "I'm fine. Work's busy, but that's nothing new. I still love my job. If you want to come visit, just give me a little notice so I can ask for time off when you're here."

"I'll check with your dad tomorrow and we'll email some dates. I know you love your job and Diamond Creek's about as beautiful a place as you can find, but do you have any friends? I…"

Violet sensed her mother was about to say she worried about that, so she cut her off. "Mom, you don't need to worry about my social life. I'm making friends. It's slow but steady. In fact, you'll be happy to know I joined one of the local baseball teams this weekend."

"Oh Violet, that's great!"

Violet bit her lip to keep from laughing. She was lucky. She had two parents who loved her to pieces, but they amused her at times. After being too worried to let her play sports when she was finally healthy enough to play as a child, her mother was probably ready to do cartwheels over her joining a baseball team now. She was still nervous about going, mostly because she worried about running into Sawyer. Well, worry wasn't it. No, rather she wanted to see him so desperately she didn't know what to do about it. She batted that thought away and focused on her conversation.

"You don't have to get so excited, Mom. I'm glad I'm trying it out, but it's not like I'm sitting around by myself."

Another sigh from her mother. "You know,

could you just let me care? Just a little about how you're doing? I know you don't like that we were overprotective after you got sick, but we were just stumbling along. If I could go back and not be a mother hen, I would. But I can't. You were very sick for a while, and we were scared. These days, it's different because they know all about how to treat leukemia, and they're much more confident about recovery rates. Back then, we were terrified. Honestly, even today we would be. It's scary for a parent to hear their child has cancer. You're healthy as a horse now, and I feel so blessed. Back to my point though, this isn't all about me. You're so brave and strong, but you turn it against yourself sometimes. It's okay to let people worry. You don't talk about it much, but I know what happened with Ted was awful. I know you wanted to have children. Even if you end up adopting, it's still something you had to let go of. So while you're busy being my amazing, strong, and brave daughter, don't forget to let people in. That's all I'm saying."

Violet was stunned into silence. With sudden clarity, she recognized her mother's point. She'd had to push so hard against their worry that she hated when anyone worried about her. She always had to be strong, never vulnerable. Sawyer flashed into her mind. When she practically ran away from him the other night, it was her internal sense of vulnerability that drove her. Her body's out-of-control need for him frightened her and made her feel way too exposed. She was quiet long enough, her mother spoke again.

"Violet? Honey, I didn't mean…"

"It's okay, Mom. I think you might be right," she said softly. "Let's make a deal, you can be worried for five minutes every week when we talk."

Her mother's soft laugh made her smile. "Okay, deal." She heard a sound in the background and then her mother's voice again. "Hon, Mrs. Wellington across the hall needs help with her groceries. Do you mind if I go?"

"Of course not! Tell her I said hi."

"You got it. Love you," her mother said quickly, clicking the line off so fast Violet's return reply was lost and she found herself telling an empty line she loved her.

Violet slowly set her phone down and stared out over the view. It was early evening with the sun slowly dipping down the sky, subtle streaks of pink illuminating the jagged mountain peaks in the distance. Boats were coming into the harbor, crowding the area of the bay outside Otter Cove Harbor. She wondered how Sawyer was doing. He should've had his surgery today. She'd recalled that this morning on her way to work.

She swung away from the windows and walked to the refrigerator, opening it to stare inside. With few choices for dinner, she grabbed her purse and phone on the way out to the grocery store. She needed something to eat and something to do. She didn't like thinking about Sawyer because she didn't know what to do about him. She wished she didn't like him so damn much. A fun fling wouldn't be a bad thing for her. It might even be a good thing, but she didn't think she could trick herself into thinking anything with Sawyer was just a fling.

CHAPTER 10

Sawyer leaned back into the sofa in Gage and Marley's living room and carefully eased his leg onto the ottoman Marley had set in front of him. Once he was settled, he looked out the windows and shook his head. It was hard to believe they looked at this every day. They lived in private quarters above the lodge restaurant. He remembered visiting his grandparents here many, many years ago before the lodge closed up. Gage and Marley had renovated this area, just as they had the rest of the lodge. The bones of the space were the same with an expansive living room and kitchen with a wall of windows that looked out over the mountains behind the lodge. Kachemak Bay was visible to the far edge of the view. At the moment, the ski slopes were grassy and green, although people still dotted the area with hikers and bikers using the area. Gage had wisely created a series of interconnected trails for use outside of ski season. He'd also established business relationships with a few local businesses for chartered fishing and flightseeing, which meant the lodge stayed busy year-round.

"Anything to drink?" Marley called from the kitchen.

"I'll take whatever you have," he replied.

The door opened, and he glanced over his shoulder to see Gage walking in with Sawyer's favorite niece, Holly, at his side. Gage's hand dwarfed Holly's where he held it. She immediately let go and ran toward the couch. "Saw!" she said with a giggle. At one and a half years old, Holly's limited vocabulary was expanding by leaps and bounds, but she'd called Sawyer 'Saw' ever since she could talk at all. He hoped she never stopped because he loved it.

"Hey Holly-girl!" he called out as she ran over to him. With her auburn hair getting darker and her bright green eyes, she was a ringer for her mother.

Gage caught up to her in two swift strides and hooked his hand in the hood of her sweatshirt. She came to a jolting stop and turned to glare at him. Gage was unperturbed by his toddler's annoyance. "Remember, Uncle Saw is getting better. No jumping on him. Got it?"

Holly looked back at Sawyer and then to her father again before nodding vigorously. "No jumping," she agreed.

As soon as Gage released her hood, Holly walked at a slower, wobbly pace. Her grin was infectious. She started to climb onto the couch beside him, but slipped, so he held his hand out and gave her a tug. She settled beside him and patted his arm. "Saw," she said affectionately.

Marley stepped around the island in the kitchen, which served as a divider between the kitchen and living room, and stopped beside Gage. He dipped his head and dropped a kiss on her neck, saying something so softly Sawyer couldn't hear it. He didn't doubt it was an endearment. Gage was ridiculously in love with Marley. When Sawyer first heard about it, he'd been skeptical. Gage had generally not taken the time to worry about relationships. Sawyer had to eat crow and admit he'd been flat wrong to doubt any of it. Marley was about the best thing to happen to Gage after he left his career as a Navy SEAL behind him.

Sawyer couldn't help but wonder if something similar was possible for him. Violet immediately came to mind, and he wondered again what lay behind her mixed responses to him. Before he had a chance to dwell, Marley walked to the sofa and ran her hand through Holly's soft hair. "Hey sweetie, did you have fun at G's?" she asked.

'G' was Garrett. Gage had taken Holly with him on a few errands and left her at Garrett's office for a little bit. Holly nodded enthusiastically. "Uh huh."

Marley grinned and looked up at Sawyer. "So, what'll it be? Water, coffee, juice?"

Gage hung his jacket on the hooks by the door and kicked off his boots before walking to the sectional couch and plunking down at an angle from Sawyer. "I say beer. It's…" he glanced at his watch. "…after five. Wait, are you allowed to drink beer?" he asked, looking to Sawyer.

"Uh, yeah. Why wouldn't I be?"

"I don't know. Because of your painkillers or something."

"Not taking any. I hate those damn things. They make me feel all out of it. I used them for the first two days after the surgery and that's it. Ibuprofen is good enough. Honestly, aside from the soreness, the pain is actually better than it was before the surgery. Those bits of shrapnel were damn painful."

Gage cracked a grin. "Damn glad to hear it. Well, if you're up for a beer, I am."

"Sounds good."

Gage glanced up to Marley who'd started to walk back toward the kitchen. "Need me to get it, babe? You don't have to wait on us."

Marley laughed and shook her head. "I've got it. It's not waiting on you if you do it for me as much as I do you. Plus, let me fuss over Sawyer a little. He could use it."

Gage threw his head back with a laugh. "That's what I told him. Speaking of that, how's Violet?" he asked with a sly look at Sawyer.

Holly clambered off the couch and made a beeline for her toy basket over by the windows. Sawyer watched her when he replied, trying to keep his tone casual. "I wouldn't know. She canceled on me last time."

"What about the other night? I'm no expert but she sure seemed into you from what I could tell."

Sawyer looked to Gage just as Marley arrived with two beers in hand. Handing them off to each of them, she sat down beside Gage. "Agreed. I don't know Violet all that well, but chemistry is hard to ignore. You two certainly have it," Marley said with a grin.

Sawyer shrugged. "Maybe so, but she took off as soon as you guys left. Haven't heard from her since."

Marley looked genuinely confused. "Really?"

Sawyer nodded. "Really."

Marley pursed her lips and stared at him, long enough it made Sawyer want to squirm a little.

"What?" he finally asked.

Marley shrugged. "I don't know. I guess I'm wondering what you want. If you ask me, it sounds like she's spooked. Which makes sense if she's really into you, but trying to be realistic about the fact you don't even live here. I mean, I'm not saying you two are destined for happily-ever-after and all that, but I know if I hadn't been sure of where Gage meant to stay, I probably would've steered clear. It's not exactly fun to fall for someone and try to be prepared for them to leave. Maybe she's not up for a fling? Because that's how she'd have to think of it not knowing how long you'll be around."

Sawyer absorbed Marley's words and knew she was spot on. Problem was, he didn't know what he was doing either. He was relieved to have his surgery over, yet now the path to a decision had a timetable.

"Where you at with what's next anyway?" Gage asked presciently.

Most of the time, Sawyer loved his family. He knew he was blessed to have a family that cared enough to be nosy. Yet, sometimes it was annoying. Particularly when he didn't know what the hell to do. His career had been one of clear decisions. He'd known before he graduated from high school that he planned to go into the Navy. He'd done exactly that and gotten his college degree while he was at it. Once that was done, he kept moving through the steps to become a Navy SEAL, driven by clear thinking and confidence in his abilities. Years as a Navy SEAL had only reinforced all of that.

He glanced to his leg, which really was feeling better. Those bits of shrapnel that had been causing the chronic pain in his knee and leg were gone with nothing but lingering soreness from the surgical incisions left behind. The surgeon had been bluntly honest after the surgery, telling him he needed to be prepared for his knee to never quite make it back to where it had once been. Not because of the shrapnel, but due to the fractured femur that had already been operated on. As for function, that meant he'd be lagging in the speed and reflexes he needed to be on active duty as a SEAL, which meant if he didn't choose to make a formal career change, he'd be doing admin duty. He was pretty sure he'd hate that. Hence, it was decision time.

He looked back at Gage and shrugged. "Dunno. Still trying to sort it out."

Gage's hand was resting behind Marley's shoulders, and he idly sifted his fingers through her hair. Oddly, that small gesture, which Sawyer doubted Gage was even thinking about, hit Sawyer hard. Blazing hot attraction to Violet aside, he wouldn't mind having that kind of comfort and intimacy with someone.

"What are your chances to go back to active duty?" Gage asked, his eyes sharp and serious.

"Not good. I have to pretty much decide if I want to suck it up and do admin duty."

"Don't man. It's akin to watching paint dry. Thought I was gonna lose my mind. Take your medical retirement and stay here."

Sawyer hated admitting it, but he didn't like the term medical retirement. It made him feel old and useless. He knew perfectly well he wasn't. He was still in peak condition. All he had was a single knee that affected the elite skill set he needed to be on active duty, but still.

Demonstrating his mind-reading abilities, Gage said, "Don't be stupid and think it means anything else. You've put in ten years there. You've done more for your country than most will ever even consider. Not much higher for you to go in your career."

Sawyer took a breath and let it out slowly, chuckling when he noticed Holly's expression when the blocks she'd been stacking tumbled over. She glared at them as if they'd personally hurt her and then promptly got back to work. He looked back to Gage. "I know. Just have to get used to the idea."

"While you're getting used to it, how about you find Violet and make sure she knows you won't be running off?" Gage asked with a wink.

Sawyer took a pull from his beer and rolled his eyes, feigning casual even if he knew damn well his feelings for Violet ran deeper. His family's nosiness annoyed him just enough he didn't feel like playing along. "You act like it's a done deal me staying here."

Marley grinned. "I'm willing to bet on it."

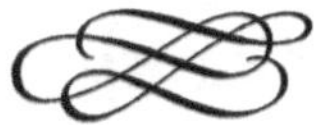

CHAPTER 11

*V*iolet watched as a baseball came flying at Ginger. With a resounding crack, Ginger connected the bat with the ball and took off running. Garrett ran to snag the ball when it thumped to the ground behind him at third base. In a flash, he sent it flying to Nick at second base who caught it just before Ginger reached the base. She skidded to a stop and gave Nick a high-five before returning to first base. At nine years old, Nick was quite the player, at least as far as Violet could tell. She was watching her new team, the Diamond Creek Batters, practice. Ginger had tried to insist Violet play today, but after Violet explained she didn't even know the rules of baseball, Ginger acceded and agreed perhaps watching a few practices might be wise.

Violet was sitting in the dugout due to a vicious wind this afternoon. The sky was bright blue with the sun high. She'd learned in her short time in Alaska that clear skies often meant windy days. Even in the sheltered area of the dugout, she shivered when a gust blasted through sideways. She tugged her jacket closer together and watched when Gage stepped up to bat. As she'd have expected, Gage sent the ball sailing far out of reach.

Nick, being the hustler he was, took off running. Garrett called out," Hey buddy, don't waste your time."

Violet jumped when a voice came from her side. "That's Garrett, always efficient."

She glanced up to see Sawyer ducking under the side of the dugout. He sat down on the bench beside her, not too close and not too far. Just close enough to make her wish two things at once. She wanted him to be closer, so she could savor the electricity that hummed to life whenever he was near. She also wanted him to move further away, far enough that she could feel in control of her body. She gave herself a mental shake. *Act normal. Sawyer's just a man. Oh, really? Not many men, none to be exact, get you so hot and bothered you keep dreaming about them.*

Another mental shake and Violet forced herself to focus on the moment. What the hell had Sawyer just said? Oh right. Something about Garrett. "What do you mean?" she asked because she didn't actually recall what he'd said.

"Garrett's the master of efficiency. He won't chase that ball because it'd be a waste of time. No matter how fast Nick runs, the distance to reach the ball and get back to second base is farther than the distance Gage needs to run to reach home," Sawyer said just as Gage reached home base. Then Sawyer smiled, his dreamy gray eyes locking onto hers.

Her breath caught and her pulse went wild. Oh dear God. She had to get a grip on her body somehow. Her body immediately proved she had no choice. Butterflies danced in her belly and heat suffused her. She swallowed and tried to take a breath, but only managed a shallow one. Fine. She'd at least try to carry on a normal conversation.

"I wouldn't have even thought to gauge the distance." She paused, suddenly recalling he'd had surgery since she last saw him. "How'd the surgery go?" She hadn't been paying close attention when he stepped into the dugout, so she didn't even know if he had a limp.

"Great. No complications," he said with a firm nod.

"I never asked what the surgery was for. I knew it was for your knee, but that's it."

"Got too close for comfort to an IED in Iraq. They did emergency surgery in the field, but they missed a few bits of shrapnel. I had to wait until they got the cast off from my fractured femur. They cleared me for this follow up surgery last month."

She knew he was a Navy SEAL and knew what that meant, but somehow hearing him speak so matter-of-factly about his injury hit her hard. She looked to him and felt tears welling. His eyes widened slightly, and he slid closer to her. "Hey, I'm fine. Seriously. Better than I've been in months."

She swallowed against the tightness in her throat and nodded. "Sorry. It's just weird to think about what you do. I'm glad you're okay." She managed another breath and felt the threat of tears ease.

Sawyer nodded somberly. "Right. Guess it sounds heavy sometimes, and it is." There was a long pause and then he shrugged. "Won't be running up against any more IED's though. I'll be taking my medical retirement and staying here."

She smiled, a rush of joy rolling through her. She shouldn't be so damn happy about this because no matter how much she wanted Sawyer, she needed to keep things casual. There were too many complications any other way she looked at it. At the moment, she didn't think about any of that and just beamed at him. "Really?"

He nodded, a small smile playing at the corners of his mouth. "Yeah. I've been tossing it around for months and finally decided if I was dreading admin duty that much, I'd best take matters into my own hands. Ten years in the SEAL's is plenty. I loved every minute of it. Even when things didn't go right..."

"Like with the IED?"

"Even then. Everything we did meant something and that's not always easy to find. But it's time for a change. I love my family and most of 'em are here now. Gage has all kinds of plans for the lodge. I might do more than that, but it's a place to start."

He was watching her, and she sensed he was trying to climb right inside her brain. She almost laughed aloud because if he could see inside her mind, he'd probably think she was crazy. With sheer force of will, she kept her mind on the actual conversation. "Wow. That's a big decision."

He shrugged. "Yes and no. In the military, either you decide to stay for good, or not. Ten years is good for me. Took me a bit to make up my mind. Probably because I'd rather have walked out instead of limped out," he offered with a grin.

"You won't be limping for long," she said with an encouraging smile.

His eyes crinkled at the corners when he smiled again. "Nah. Told Garrett I'd run with him in some Mount Marathon race around here. No idea what he's talking about, but give me a few months and I'll be ready."

A vicious gist of wind blew sideways through the dugout. When Violet unconsciously shivered, Sawyer slipped his arm over her shoulders. "Damn cold for a summer day," he commented.

She couldn't help but love having him close. She could feel the corded muscles of his arm through her windbreaker, and he was like her personal furnace. In seconds, the wind didn't feel so cold. Oh hell. She'd be happy to sit here all day now. The part of her that was resisting her wild, uncontrollable attraction to Sawyer was weary. She didn't feel like fighting with herself right now. She'd tensed up when he put his arm around her, but she relaxed against his side after a moment.

Casting about for something to say, she stared out over the baseball field. Delia was up to bat now with Nick pitching to her. From Violet's vast experience of watching the team practice, she'd discovered they casually rotated which players covered what position. Nick seemed to be pretty good at pitching from what she could gather. He threw two strikes, but Delia connected with the third pitch and sent the ball sailing into the outfield.

"Damn good hit," Sawyer said.

She glanced up. "Seeing as I've had basically zero experience, I've got no comparison. Are they pretty good?"

"Oh yeah. Gage and I played baseball all through school. Garrett's got the speed, and he's a damn good batter. Everyone else is pretty darn good. You seriously planning on playing?"

"Uh huh. I want to. I might be terrible at it, but I figure it'll be fun." She didn't say aloud how good it felt to spend time with friends. She wouldn't change a thing about moving clear across the country, but it took time to feel a part of the community and the more friends she found, the better it felt.

"Oh it will. Depending on how quickly my leg heals, I might join in by fall," he replied with another one of his devastating grins.

He really needed to stop that. Every time he looked her way, her low belly clenched and heat slid through her veins. When he smiled, the heat amped up a notch inside.

His smile slowly faded as she looked up at him. Another gust of wind blew a lock of hair loose from her ponytail. He reached up with his free hand and brushed it out of her eyes. When he tucked it behind her ear, a hot shiver chased in the wake of his touch. She couldn't look away as his eyes darkened to a smoky gray. With her pulse racing, she stared back at him. He was only inches away, and she was nearly frantic for him to close the distance. She craved the feel of his lips on hers again. His eyes searched hers as if he was wondering something.

He cleared his throat. "Tell me, Violet: what do you want?"

So lost in the desire pounding through her, she didn't even think before she spoke. "To kiss you," she blurted out.

His eyes darkened further. "And after that?"

he asked, his hand sliding into her hair to cup the nape of her neck. His thumb stroked in slow passes on the sensitive skin behind her ear.

With her belly somersaulting and her pulse thundering, wet heat built between her thighs. Her thoughts were fuzzy, and it was hard to focus, but she forced herself to try. "What do you mean?"

"Never mind. I can't think until *this*," he nearly growled as he closed the distance between them and crushed his lips to hers.

Their kiss exploded, a tangle of lips teeth and tongue. For Violet, it had been far too long since she'd tumbled into the madness that was kissing Sawyer. After a fierce beginning, he eased back, his tongue gliding against hers in a slow pass before he drew her bottom lip between his teeth and gave it a tug. He traced her lips with his tongue, while she frantically struggled to get closer to him. To be specific, she shifted and straddled him, sighing with relief when she sank her hips down and felt the hard, hot length of his shaft against her. The layers of her leggings and his jeans didn't do much to hide his arousal.

She was burning up inside. Everything around them faded away—the sounds of laughter and voices carrying across the baseball field, the thwack of the bat connecting with the baseball—and her entire reality narrowed to the feel of him against her. Under her windbreaker, she wore a V-neck t-shirt. Sawyer shoved her jacket apart and slipped his hands around her waist, one palm sliding up her spine in a heated pass and the other easing around to trail his fingers under the curves of her breasts. Her nipples were tight and achy.

Her own hands were busy pushing his jacket out of the way. She sighed at the feel of his muscled chest. Every inch of him was hard muscle. She moaned when he tore his lips free and blazed a searing path of kisses down her neck. With a muttered swear he yanked on her shirt, the cotton giving way and exposing one of her breasts. His mouth closed over her nipple, soaking the silk of her bra. She cried out and gripped his hair. She didn't realize she was rolling her hips against him until he lifted his head swiftly. "Damn. Vi, we have to…"

His voice was strained as he gripped her hips and held her still. He pinned her with a fierce, hot gaze. With need roaring through her, its flames licking inside, she stared back at him, scrambling for purchase in her mind.

"We have to stop," he said, his voice gruff.

His body belied his voice when he arched his hips into hers, sending a spike of pleasure through her. She licked her lips.

"Oh hell. You can't do that," he murmured, his voice pained.

"Why…?"

Just as she was about to ask why they had to stop, cheers from the field beyond the dugout filtered into her awareness. She glanced over her shoulder to see Nick skidding into home base. She'd completely forgotten where they were. Mortified, she spun back. "Oh God. I wasn't thinking…"

She started to scramble off his lap, but his hands held her in place. "Good to know I'm not the only one who can't think when we're together. Don't suppose we could try dinner again?"

Violet tried to think clearly, but she couldn't. All she knew was she wanted this moment to never end, but it wasn't like she could tear Sawyer's clothes off right here with a bunch of people nearby. The next best thing would be to see him again, somewhere, sometime when they didn't have to stop.

She nodded. His mouth curled at one corner. She started to wiggle off of him again, worried someone would come over and see her straddling him. He shook his head. "Not until you tell me when. I'd prefer tonight if I get to pick."

She heard Ginger say something and nodded quickly. "Tonight sounds good," she managed.

He eased his hold on her, but not before arching his hips into hers again. Her body in thrall of him, she reflexively rolled her hips, biting back a cry at the sweet streak of pleasure that rolled through her. She managed to scramble off his lap and pull her clothes into place, seconds before Ginger walked to the dugout and leaned over to look inside.

"Come on, Violet. Why don't you at least try to bat once today?"

Hot, flushed and restless, Violet leapt up from the bench. Sawyer followed her out and stood nearby with Gage, while Ginger gave her a few pointers. The practice had moved on from organized play to clusters of people practicing throwing, catching and batting. Violet surprised herself with a solid hit the first time Nick, her assigned pitcher, pitched the ball her way. The thwack of the ball against the bat was surprisingly satisfying. Beaming, she glanced to Ginger who'd coached her through the swing.

"See! I knew you could do it!" Ginger gave her a thumbs up and looked to Nick, immediately all business again. "Okay, Nick, give her another nice, easy throw."

Not much later, Violet had successfully hit several of the pitches thrown her way when the group broke up for the evening. Ginger paused at her side while everyone was gathering up bats, balls and gloves. "You think you're ready for a game?"

Before this afternoon, she'd have emphatically said no. Now, after discovering that the team was lighthearted and obviously just wanted to have some fun, she nodded. "Yup. I can handle it. I don't think you should have me do anything other than be a back up. I might be able to hit the ball, but Nick was making it super easy for me."

Ginger grinned. "Yay! Okay, we play every Thursday night at six right here. See you then." With a wave, she jogged off when Cam called her name.

Violet glanced around to see if there was anything left to do before making her way back toward the parking lot. She reached her car to find Sawyer leaning against it. Just standing there, he made her mouth water and her belly do flips all over again. Lounging against her car, his t-shirt pulled tight across his muscled chest and his faded black jeans hugged his muscled legs. The angle of the setting sun cast his face in shadow, illuminating his chiseled features. He screamed strong and sexy, and she wanted to eat him up. On the short walk to the parking lot, she'd wondered where he'd gone and then berated herself for getting worried he'd forgotten about asking her to dinner.

You don't even know what you want and you're all gaga over this guy. Pump the brakes, girl. That was one part of her brain. Another part of her brain had different ideas. *Oh, you know what you want. Sawyer. Naked. Now.*

CHAPTER 12

Sawyer watched Violet as she approached him. He concluded he should win a damn award for managing to keep himself from tearing her clothes off in the dugout. The remainder of the afternoon hadn't exactly helped. Violet was too tempting. She'd worn these leggings that accentuated her generous hips. He figured she'd worn them to be practical, along with her simple V-neck t-shirt, but when it came to Violet, everything was distracting.

She reached him and glanced up, her cheeks going rosy pink when she met his eyes. Her dark hair fell loosely around her shoulders. Somewhere along the way, she'd tugged the elastic holding it in place off after a blast of wind. His body ran on high idle whenever she was near. One look into her eyes, into that translucent blue he could lose himself in, and lust jolted him. She'd tied her windbreaker around her waist and twirled one of the loose sleeves in her hand. Biting her lip, she said, "Well, I wasn't sure if you still wanted to have dinner."

Sometime he'd have to tell her not to bite her lip, at least not in public. Her mouth was nearly perfect—full, lush lips. Without even a bit of makeup, they were so pink and tempting against her creamy complexion, it was all he could do not to yank her to him and pour his pent up desire into another kiss. Yet, a kiss wouldn't be enough and he damn well knew it. He knew a lot of things, but one thing he didn't know was what the hell to do with this almost electric attraction he felt for Violet. He'd managed to make a reasoned decision about staying in Diamond Creek and had mostly convinced himself he wouldn't care one way or the other if Violet gave him a shot.

Then, he saw her again this afternoon. If he were being honest, he'd come to baseball practice because he knew she might be here. He could pretend it was because his family was here too, but that was a flat lie. He'd wanted any chance he could find to run into her again. He was usually a man with a plan, yet at the moment he had none. He could only think as far ahead as the next step. Right now, he had to get through dinner when all he really wanted was to find somewhere private and let himself be consumed by the burning need Violet elicited inside him. After that, well, he had no clue what it all meant.

He realized he was doing nothing other than staring at Violet when she cocked her head to the side, her eyes holding a silent question. What the hell had she just said? Dinner. Something about dinner. "Of course I still want to have dinner," he said. Dinner was the avenue to more, so he'd take it.

She glanced at her watch and then back to him. "It's almost six now. Should I meet you somewhere in a little bit?"

Knowing that the last time there'd been any time for her to second guess, she had, Sawyer wasn't about to let it happen again.

"How about now?"

Her gorgeous eyes widened and something flashed in their depths. After a moment, she nodded. "Okay. Um, where do you want to go?"

He had no idea. All he wanted was time with her. He said the first thing that came to mind. "How about something simple, like pizza?"

Violet smiled. "Pizza's perfect. I'm starving. Do you want to follow me?"

"How about you drop your car off, and we'll ride together from there?"

His suggestion was practical because her apartment was close by. Yet, it was also selfish. He didn't want to give her a chance to leave him behind. He wasn't so far gone that he'd push her past boundaries she didn't want to blow through. But he knew what he felt when she kissed him. No matter the reasons behind her canceling on him last week, he knew she wanted him. The chemistry between them was explosive. He shied away from wondering about her mixed reactions to him and focused on what he felt. That itself was odd because his entire career as a Navy SEAL was built on not letting his emotions get the best of him. Yet, those illusive factors, such as emotion, his visceral response to her and more, were what drove him and the only thing that made sense.

A gust of wind blew her hair in a swirl, and Violet brushed a few loose locks out of her eyes before nodding. "Okay."

She stood there, her gaze expectant. After a moment, she gestured to her car. "Don't suppose you'll move so I can get in," she said with a sly grin.

He grinned. "Ah. That would make sense, huh?" He pushed away from her car and opened the door for her. "Be right behind you."

* * *

VIOLET FIDDLED WITH HER NAPKIN, neatly folding it into a square and smoothing it against the table before taking a healthy gulp of her wine. Sawyer had left the booth to go to the restroom before they left. Dinner had turned out to be a continuation of the long, slow tease of the afternoon. She was coming to realize she was kidding herself if she thought she could get a grip on her attraction to Sawyer. It was like a horse galloping out of control. She had no reins and could do nothing other than hold on. After their kiss in the dugout, she'd managed to distract herself learning to bat, but even then her thoughts had been half on Sawyer most of the time. While waiting, she glanced around the restaurant.

After his request for pizza, she'd suggested the local favorite place in town, Glacier Pizza.

It stayed busy year-round, however in the summer it was bustling, as was every place in town. They'd arrived to wait in line before being seated, and a line had remained the entire time they'd been there. The décor was simple with the only decorations being photos from locals and tourists, along with license plates from all over the country. A brick oven was situated in the center with an open kitchen circling around it. A counter surrounding the kitchen and booths lining the walls provided the seating. The atmosphere was relaxed and bustling at once. The restaurant also had amazing pizza. Being from New York, Violet was accustomed to heated debates over what constituted good pizza. She'd wager Glacier Pizza could hold its own in New York.

Sawyer emerged from the hallway that led to the restrooms, and her low belly clenched. She felt as if she was about to melt inside. Restless, she crossed and uncrossed her legs. His limp was minimal, and damn if he didn't manage to look sexy as all hell just walking across the restaurant. His muscled arms swung with his stride. Her eyes hungrily tracked him as he made his way to her. She'd given up fighting against the need simmering inside of her because it made her weary and annoyed with herself. She didn't know what she intended to do, but she thought perhaps maybe she'd get her footing back if she let herself have what she so badly wanted. Or rather who.

Sawyer stopped beside the booth, glancing down at her. He'd paid the bill before he stepped away. He didn't say a word, merely arched a dark brow. "Shall we? I'm guessing if we don't clear out soon, they'll just have someone join us," he said with a grin as he nodded his head toward the entrance where a cluster of people were waiting for tables to open up.

Moments later, they were walking outside into the late evening. It was past nine and the sun's descent behind the mountains left a fiery blaze in its wake. The sky was streaked with orange and red shot through with gold. The mountains across the bay were dark against the backdrop and the water shimmered brightly, reflecting the sky's colors. Somehow she managed to put one foot in front of the other and walk to Sawyer's truck. Her body was humming with need, and she was hot all over. The short drive to her apartment, which was only minutes from Glacier Pizza, was quiet. The air inside the truck felt heavy and taut, weighted with the depth of desire between them.

By the time Sawyer parked his truck by the stairs leading up to her apartment, Violet was flat annoyed with herself. She wasn't this wishy-washy woman who was all a muddle because of a man. She was better than that. If she were going to face this head on, she'd do it on her terms. She might not particularly like how she couldn't control her rampaging need for Sawyer, but she could either be twisted and turned in its force, or grab ahold of it and make it her own.

There were a few things she couldn't have, but she could let herself dive into this wild, crackling attraction and enjoy it for all it was worth. She'd worry about the rest later. Without a word, she climbed out of the truck.

Sawyer had followed her out of the truck, his gaze watchful. She didn't wait and started walking up the stairs. The office building downstairs had a front entrance, while a set of stairs led to a small deck and the entrance to her apartment on the side of the building. Sawyer's tread sounded behind her after a moment, and she stopped at the top of the stairs to turn to face him.

He paused a step below her, their faces almost level, although even then he was still taller than her. She guessed him to top six feet plus. She stared into his smoky gray eyes, her pulse rocketing and her breath shallow. He searched her face, his gaze considering. He started to say something, but stopped when she stepped closer. The heat emanating from him sent a hot shiver through her. It was chilly out now with the wind still gusting off the bay.

"You're coming in," she said.

"Am I now?" he countered, his eyes darkening.

With her pulse thundering in her ears, she nodded, grabbing onto the bold side of herself. "Yes. You're driving me crazy, so I'm doing something about it." At that, she shuffled a step closer, her breasts brushing against his chest, and slipped a hand around his neck as she brought her lips to his. The delicious contrast of the chilled air and the heat of his body was a shock to her system. The relief at finally giving in to the need consuming her was brief. Their kiss went wild with Sawyer sliding his arms around her waist and pulling her flush against him. She might have started as the aggressor, but he flipped the script in a flash. One palm slid up her spine and tangled in her hair, angling her head to the side as he devoured her mouth, his tongue stroking boldly against hers. His other hand cupped her bottom and tugged her against him, the hard ridge of his cock pressing against her. She moaned in his mouth when he flexed into her, creating just enough pressure against her clit that a jolt of pleasure zinged through her.

He tore his lips free, the abrupt end of their kiss startling her eyes open. She found his waiting, the desire in his gaze so frank, she flushed. She moved to catch his lips again, but he shook his head. "I need to know something," he said, his gruff voice sending a shudder through her.

"What?" she said, her own voice raspy and breathy.

"Are you planning to chase me off again?"

Not caring to contemplate his question, she shook her head. A distant warning bell rang in the back of her mind, but she didn't want to heed anything other than her yearning need for Sawyer right now.

His eyes searched hers, the air around them fairly cracking with the raw electricity of their desire. He nodded, almost as if to himself. Then, he sifted his fingers through her hair and trailed them down the side of her neck. Goose bumps rose all over her skin, and she shivered. His touch was almost too much. She grabbed his hand in hers and spun away, all but dragging him behind her.

In seconds, they'd stumbled inside. Her purse and keys clattered to the floor when he slammed the door shut behind them and spun her around. His mouth collided with hers as he backed her against the door. Their kiss picked up right where it left off, only this time it was hotter, deeper and so overpowering, she could barely breathe. When he broke free and his lips blazed down the column of her throat, she gulped in air.

She was twined around him, all but frantic to meld herself to him. Every inch of him was hard muscle and she loved it, sweet hell did she love it. He abruptly stepped back and yanked at her shirt. Cool air rushed over her skin when he tossed it aside. He paused, his eyes locking to hers, and she thought she might come just from the look in his eyes. Her panties were soaked, and her channel throbbed. After an electric moment, he spoke.

"I'd love to fuck you right here against the door, but I don't want to rush this. Bedroom," he said.

Her knees weak from the look in his eyes, she pressed a palm against the door and pushed herself off, walking straight across the living room to the bedroom in the back. She kicked her shoes off on the way and heard his thump to the floor behind her as she tossed her shirt and bra to the floor. She managed to flick a lamp on before he stroked a palm down her back. She stumbled to a stop where she stood at the foot of the bed. She started to turn around but he slowly slipped his hands around her waist, reaching to hook his hands over the waistband of her leggings and shoving them down quickly.

In a flash, Violet was stretched out on the bed with Sawyer's palms sliding up her legs, his gaze so hot she could hardly bear it. When his palms reached her thighs, he paused. She looked up at him. "Not fair."

He arched a brow in question.

She sat up quickly and yanked at his t-shirt. "You're still dressed."

His low chuckle sent a wave of heat through her. She had it bad and she didn't care anymore. He accommodated her and stood, reaching behind his head and pulling his shirt off quickly. She got a glimpse of his chest and abs—muscled and mouth-watering—before he curled his hands under her knees and tugged her bottom to the edge of the bed. He leaned down and stroked a finger across her panties—bright blue cotton. Nothing fancy because she tended not to bother with that. His eyes flicked up when her hips bucked into his touch. A few more passes, and she almost cried out. With one hand, he pulled her panties off and knelt between her knees.

She tried to catch her breath, but she couldn't. He dragged his fingers through her folds, which were soaked.

"You're so wet," he said. The satisfaction in his tone should've annoyed her, but it didn't. All she wanted was him inside of her.

Her breath came out in a moan as he slid one finger into her channel, sinking it deep and then sliding it back for another finger to join. Her channel throbbed around him as he set to drive her mad with steady strokes. Pleasure coiled tightly inside. Her hips rolled restlessly as she chased after release. He brought his mouth to her, and she cried out. She lost herself in a wash of sensation with his tongue and fingers driving her wild. The pressure built and built, every fiber of her being frantic for release, until he sucked her clit into his mouth and the pressure spun loose, unraveling in a burst of sharp pleasure.

He slowly eased away. She was nearly limp,

but managed to drag her eyes open to see him standing. She couldn't help but admire his efficiency as he made quick work of his jeans and tugged a condom out of his wallet before tossing it to the floor in his pile of clothes. Greedy to see him, she leaned up on her elbows. He hadn't been in elite condition in the military for over a decade without something to show for it, in this case a body so perfect, she almost sobbed. Broad shoulders, muscled chest, and abs carved from stone. As her eyes traveled down to his legs, it was impossible not to see the scarring on his left leg. Jagged shallow scars covered his upper thigh, while the distinct, surgical scars were deeper and clear to see. Her heart clenched and her eyes whipped up to his.

Even though she'd intellectually known he'd been injured, staring at the remnants of that injury made her heart ache for him. He met her gaze head on. They were silent, nothing but her ragged breathing, along with his, audible in the room. She felt an intimacy with him in that moment that she'd never known. He was a man of strength and dominance, yet she was witness to something that had threatened such an integral part of him.

The percussive beat of her heart pounded

through her body as he slowly stretched out over her. It felt so good, so damn good to feel his weight over her, his strength and heat surrounding her. He curled his hands over hers and stretched them up behind her head. His hips arched into hers, and she almost cried out. The feel of his cock, hard and hot, against her slick folds was almost too much. Beyond aroused, she bit her lip to keep from moaning when he rocked into her.

"Vi."

His voice was gruff. Opening her eyes, she was instantly caught in his smoky gaze, intent and focused solely on her. He was still for a few beats, the pause serving only to ratchet up her need. She found it hard to believe she was already desperate for release again, having just had an explosive orgasm. But she was. Nothing had been enough yet, so she needed him inside of her. She curled her legs around his hips.

"Sawyer," she whispered roughly. "Don't make me keep waiting."

His eyes flashed. She could feel his heart pounding against her breasts, but he made her wait just long enough, she arched into him. He adjusted the angle of his hips and sank home in a swift surge. Her cry was raw and throaty and mingled with his low groan. He held still for a long moment as her channel adjusted to his size. Since her choice to eschew relationships, she'd gone a good two years without actual sex. Her channel was tight, and he had plenty to fill her with. The delicious stretch of his cock was almost enough to send her over the edge again. After a moment, he drew away and slid back inside, settling into a slow, maddening rhythm. Every time she bucked roughly into him, urging him on, he simply kept up the relentless, steady drive into her. Pleasure whipped through her, as she teetered on the edge of another release. His hands gripped hers tightly and stretched her arms further up, her body naturally arching up in response.

"Sawyer, please…"

She couldn't even finish whatever she'd meant to say because he went from slow to pounding and sent her flying. Tremors wracked her body as pleasure ripped through her. His grip tightened and his body went rigid before he cried out and collapsed against her. His forehead fell against hers. They lay still like that—joined as deeply as two human beings could be joined, their breath mingling, and their sweat cooling.

Somehow they untangled themselves and stumbled into the shower. Violet didn't want to think, so after they dried off, she slipped her hand in his and tugged him back into bed. She fell asleep curled up against him, savoring his heat and strength, and ignoring the distant warning bells clanging in her brain.

CHAPTER 13

Sawyer leaned an elbow on the bar in the lodge restaurant and glanced to Gage. "You think we should start our own guide business?" he asked.

It was early afternoon and the restaurant was quiet, although there were a few customers scattered about. He'd learned this was a time of day when Gage often handled the business end of things, either in his office, or at the bar when he had a late lunch. Gage finished a bite of his burger and nodded. After a swallow of water, he clarified, "I do. I've got some great working partnerships with a few local places, but they're all so damn busy people are often waitlisted. I mean, Eli's so busy he can barely see straight all summer," he said, in reference to Jessa's husband who ran a backcountry guiding and charter business, along with the retail store that provided all the gear needed for such trips.

"Aren't you worried about butting in on his territory? I mean, he's family," Sawyer said.

Gage finished off the last bite of his burger, while Sawyer nibbled on some chips. "Nah. He'd love it if we ran a few of our own trips. So would the Winters' brothers who help us out as well. I don't want this to be a primary business, and we won't do any fishing charters. It would be something we only offer customers staying at the lodge. I've been tossing it around for a while, but I haven't had time. Cam could handle any backcountry ski trips for people crazy enough to want to do that," he said. Cam was a world-class skier who'd landed in Diamond Creek after his brother died. He was a draw for visitors looking for serious ski instruction and was a huge help to Gage otherwise at the lodge. "I figure you and I can handle any of the hikes and whatnot. It's not like we don't have the training," he explained, referencing the years of grueling training they'd each gone through to become Navy SEAL's and the subsequent career that often meant treks into dangerous territory, carrying loads of gear. It seemed a far cry from taking tourists out on wilderness hikes, but the skills needed were remarkably similar. If any medical emergencies arose, they were both trained to handle remote medical treatment too.

Sawyer rolled Gage's plan over in his mind and smiled slowly. "Works for me. Is this why you've been so impatient for me to decide what I was doing?"

Gage flashed a grin as he leaned back in his barstool. "Yup. I've got too much on my plate to get this going on my own, but with you here, we can think about something like this. I also didn't want to step into anything where I'd be the only one taking off. You and I can rotate who covers what trips, so I won't be gone for too long. Marley would be a good sport about it, but I hate to be away from her and Holly too much."

"All right. Can you give me a little time before we attack this plan? I need to figure out where I'm gonna live and…"

"You can stay here," Gage said quickly.

Sawyer knew he could. While he technically held part of the ownership at the lodge, this was Gage's baby. With the hard work Gage had put into bringing the lodge back to life after it had been boarded up and empty for over twenty years, well it was his to live in. There was only one set of private quarters on site, and with Gage's family settled in, Sawyer wanted it to stay that way. For a flash, he wondered what it would be like to have a family to call his own. He pictured Violet instantly. The mere thought of her sent lash of need through him. The other night with her had been so damn good, it was almost hard to think about because all it did was make him want her more.

Sawyer met Gage's gaze. "I know I can stay here, and I will until I figure out something else. Long term, it'd be nice to have my own place. Other than that, let me get my feet under me with anything else you need help with around here. To say this is a career change for me is a bit of an understatement."

Gage smiled ruefully. "Oh, I get it. Went through the same thing." He started to say something else when Don Peters walked up to them.

Don had worked for their grandparents back when they built and ran the ski lodge in its first life. He was also Delia's father and had joined Gage when he started work on the lodge a few years ago. He was an all-around helper, handling just about anything that came his way. He glanced between Gage and Sawyer. "Hey boys, I've gotta head to town to see if they have a water heater at Builders Galore. The water heater in one of the rooms broke again. This is the third time, so I'm thinking we should replace it. Anything else we need there?"

"Pick up about ten two-by-fours. I want to add a bigger closet in Holly's bedroom. You need help with the water heater?" Gage asked.

"Not yet. When I get back, if you guys could help me unload it and pull out the old one, that would be great. Your leg up for that yet?" Don asked, glancing to Sawyer.

Sawyer flexed his knee and nodded. "For the most part. It's still sore, but mostly from the incisions, instead of shrapnel rattling around in there. I can't do everything, but I can definitely be an extra set of hands to get those moved around."

Don's blue eyes crinkled with his smile in his weathered face. "Whatever you can do will be enough. I should be back in about an hour," he said as he turned and walked out into the reception area.

Gage glanced back to Sawyer. "You sure you're up to helping move those water heaters?"

"Definitely. I get why you might be worried, but this last surgery wasn't much. The hard part was when they had to put my bones back in place and I limped around in a cast for too damn long. This was just a little leftover clean up. Amazing how much a few bits of shrapnel can hurt. They're gone and the incisions are already healed up."

When Gage gave him a skeptical look, Sawyer rolled his eyes. "Dude, the surgery was arthroscopic. The incisions are tiny. I'm not planning to go running yet, but I can easily help. I'm damn relieved to finally feel close to normal again."

Gage shrugged. "If you say so. I'll trust you not to be an idiot about it."

Sawyer lightly punched him in the shoulder. "I'm never an idiot."

Gage threw his head back with a laugh. "Except for the time you thought you could push me off the dock," he said, referencing a time when Sawyer was eight years old. They'd been camping at a lake outside of Bellingham, Washington where they mostly grew up after their parents moved away from Alaska. Sawyer had seen Gage standing at the end of the dock and barreled toward him at high speed, intent on pushing him into the water. Gage, four years older and wiser, had waited until the last minute before neatly stepping to the side and watching Sawyer fly into the lake.

Sawyer chuckled. "Oh right. Except for that time. Give me some credit though, I never tried that again."

Gage clapped him on the shoulder and stood. "You sure didn't." He nodded toward Harry Lawson who stepped behind the bar to stack their plates. "You need me to carry those to the kitchen?"

Harry shook his head. "Nope. I'm headed that way in a few." Harry helped Delia run the restaurant and reception areas of the ski lodge. He was tall and thin with dark hair and brown eyes. He was almost constantly in motion and immediately spun away to tap something into the laptop mounted behind the bar.

"Will you guys be down for dinner?" he asked over his shoulder.

Gage shrugged when Harry turned back to face them. "Not sure. Depends on what Marley wants."

Harry glanced to Sawyer with a grin. "Noticed your brother is officially whipped?"

"Oh yeah. Thought it would wear off by now, but it's not looking like it," Sawyer replied with a pointed glance at Gage.

Gage was unperturbed. "Marley's the best thing that ever happened to me. No complaints here." He glanced from Harry to Sawyer and back, his eyes taking on a gleam. "Just wait until he wises up. He'll fall harder than any of us."

Harry turned his sharp, assessing gaze to Sawyer. Sawyer had already picked up that Harry noticed everything. "If you ask me, he's already on his way," Harry said with a wink.

For the first time in his life, Sawyer counted himself lucky he wasn't prone to blushing, something he'd never thought about. Ever. He didn't even want to ask how Harry knew anything about him and Violet.

Gage burst out laughing. "Can't hide anything around here."

Sawyer looked over at Harry, considering how to respond. Before he collected his thoughts, someone called Harry's name from the reception area. "Duty calls," Harry said as he rounded the end of the bar and headed to the front. He paused by the arched entrance and glanced back to Sawyer. "Violet's awesome," he said with a wink.

At that, Harry disappeared into the front, and Sawyer glanced to Gage. "How the hell does he know anything about me and Violet?"

"Dude, if Harry doesn't know something, he finds it out damn quick. What is the deal with Violet anyway? Didn't you have dinner with her again?"

Sawyer ran a hand through his hair and groaned. "Sure did. Do I need to report back to you?" he asked.

Gage grinned. "Not at all. Just curious. You're nicer when you see her."

"I've hardly seen her," he countered.

"Exactly," Gage replied.

He turned and walked out, leaving Sawyer standing there, his mind narrowed to one person—Violet.

The other night had been about the best night of his life on so many levels he almost didn't like to think about it. He wished he could chalk it up to the crazy hot chemistry he felt with Violet, but it wasn't just that and he damn well knew it. Problem was, in the cold light of day, Violet put up invisible walls. He'd woken beside her to find the sheet half off of her. He'd traced the line of her shoulder, into the swoop of her waist and up over the lush curve of her hip. Her skin was a temptation all on its own—silky soft with random freckles here and there. When she'd opened her eyes and rolled to face him, her skin went rosy all over. Her dark hair and translucent blue eyes stood out against her creamy skin. For a few seconds, she was sleepy and relaxed, the echoes of their intimacy from the night before lingering between them.

In another moment, she didn't precisely pull away, but he sensed the distance she created. She'd climbed out of bed and hurried into the shower, calling out that she had to get to work. Seeing as it had been Monday, that seemed perfectly reasonable. The next weekend was one day ahead, and Sawyer hadn't heard much from her since. She'd responded politely to his texts, but that was it.

He didn't know what the hell he meant to do, but he needed to see her. He had an hour before Don got back, so he headed out to the parking lot.

* * *

VIOLET CAREFULLY LABELED a vial of blood and stowed it in a rack in the refrigerator. She enjoyed the tidiness of having all the vials properly labeled and ready to be sent off for analysis. Another major perk to her own office was she could keep it organized the way she preferred. She had a system for every day. She spun in her chair and quickly ran through her charting to make sure everything was complete in the system. Her office phone buzzed, and she glanced at it, curious to know why reception would be buzzing her at the end of the day.

She tapped the speaker button. "Yes?"

"Jan here. A Sawyer Hamilton is on his way to your office. I couldn't find him in your schedule, but he insisted he had an appointment with you."

Violet stared at the phone, her cheeks getting hot and a flush running through her entire body. "Violet?" Jan asked.

Violet gave herself a shake. "Right. Okay. Thanks, Jan."

She couldn't bring herself to say he didn't have an appointment because Jan had already sent him her way. The one and only downside she'd discovered to living and working in a small, friendly town like Diamond Creek was people tended to assume the best of everyone. In New York, no one would ever be sent anywhere in the hospital by intake unless they knew for certain the person was supposed to be there. In Diamond Creek, Violet learned some elderly patients refused to allow their data to be entered in the electronic health record, so they had paper files—unheard of anywhere else. Jan wouldn't think twice about assuming the scheduler must've confirmed an appointment without entering it in the system. Now, Sawyer was headed her way, and she was all a muddle inside.

It had been four days since she'd seen him. Four days since he'd blown her mind and sent her body soaring to heights she'd never contemplated. Four days during which she swung between poles of longing and indecision. She wanted so much more than one night with Sawyer. But she couldn't face letting herself fall for someone again. She thought she was half-crazy for being so into him, but that's how she was. She fell, and she fell hard. She'd had to keep a leash on her desire before, but she'd never had anyone fray her control the way Sawyer did. He had special powers over her, and she needed to try to think clearly. He'd think she was nuts if she told him she needed to keep her distance because she was afraid he wanted kids someday and she'd instantly let him down if that was the case.

She quickly logged off the computer and closed her laptop. Her pulse was racing, and she was hot all over. Even while she was spinning in circles in her mind, part of her was jumping for joy. Sawyer had come to see her!

There was a sharp knock at the door. She stared at it, her heart pounding so hard it almost hurt. "Come in," she said, her voice cracking at the end.

The door opened and Sawyer stood there, his hand resting on the handle. He was quiet for a moment, his gaze coasting over her. Her skin prickled, and her breath became shallow. Still not speaking, he stepped all the way into her office and closed the door behind him. The soft click nudged her.

"Hey. I, uh, didn't know you were coming by," she said.

"I didn't either. I just decided it might be the only way to get you to talk to me," he replied. He paused, his shoulders rising and falling with a deep breath. "It's good to see you." His gruff voice sent a shiver through her.

"You too," she managed.

Oh God. This is a mess. You want him. So much. You're crazy, and you have to explain before he realizes how crazy you are. Her kinder side snapped back. *You're not crazy. You're complicated, just like everyone else.*

While her mind lobbed volleys, her emotions were a riot. She wasn't sensible when it came to Sawyer, and she'd tried so damn hard to be sensible when it came to men. She looked up into his silvery gray gaze and tried to keep breathing. Restless, she fiddled with the end of her ponytail. Back and forth, back and forth she went in her mind. She could *not* let herself get all hung up on any of her baggage. They weren't serious, nowhere close, so she needed to stop running down these crazy paths in her brain.

Twirling her ponytail in her hand, she prayed he couldn't tell what a mess she was inside.

His assessing eyes coasted over her face. He cleared his throat. "Thought I'd stop by to see if I could persuade you to have dinner with me again," he said, his expression almost boyish.

She was nodding before she realized it when she suddenly remembered she'd told Ginger she'd meet her and Delia for drinks after work. "I can't tonight though," she blurted out. The moment she nodded and spoke, she mentally kicked herself. What the hell was she thinking? Well, she wasn't, but she definitely wanted to see him again, so there was that.

The swift disappointment on his face nearly made her cheer. It wasn't that she was happy about his disappointment, but she was gratified to know he wanted to see her enough to be disappointed. Given that barely a spare moment had passed when she wasn't thinking about him, she didn't feel so alone in her state of infatuation. "I already told Ginger and Delia I'd meet them for drinks after work. Maybe tomorrow?"

"Or maybe you have drinks up at the lodge?" he countered.

Oh, he was too much. Grinning like a fool, she shook her head. "Delia specifically said she wanted to meet at the Brewery."

Sawyer shrugged. "Okay, okay. What time?"

"What time am I meeting them?"

At his nod, she replied, "Five."

He grinned. "Perfect. That's early. Mind if I join you around six-thirty?"

She blushed furiously and burst out laughing as she shook her head.

"Does that mean 'no, you don't mind,' or 'no, you do mind?'"

She caught her breath on a gasp. "I don't mind."

"Great. I'll see you then."

At that, he stood and stepped to the door. Reflexively, she stood with him and followed him to the door. He turned and glanced down at her. In a flash, the air around them hummed to life. Her pulse skittered, and heat slid through her. His eyes went smoky. They were still for several beats, the room so quiet, she feared he could hear the wild pounding of her heart.

In slow motion, he lifted a hand and caught the end of her ponytail in it, sliding his fingers through it as he tugged her to him. He dipped his head, pausing when his lips were but a whisper away from hers. "In case you forgot…"

He fit his mouth over hers, and she went up in flames inside. Inside of a nanosecond, their kiss nearly melted her—hot, wet, and over-powering. A low moan escaped when he drew back. She didn't want him to stop. At all. But he did. The lines of his face were tense as he held her gaze for a moment. On the heels of a deep breath, he stepped back, her hair slipping free from his grasp.

"See you later," he said, his voice sending a ripple through her.

She couldn't even manage a polite reply and simply watched him leave before collapsing in her chair, her pulse racing, and her panties wet.

CHAPTER 14

*V*iolet swirled the wine in her glass and laughed at the look of mock horror on Ginger's face. Delia had just finished explaining her morning, which involved a clean up project after Nick stumbled on his rush to the bathroom and threw up all over his bedroom floor.

Delia shrugged and grinned. "Hey, it could've been way worse. I'd rather clean up the floor than his bed. It's life with kids."

With her honey gold hair and blue eyes, Delia's coloring matched her generally soft demeanor. Violet was still just getting to know her, but she seemed to be a practical, caring friend. Ginger, on the other hand, was a force of wit and emotion. She caught Violet's gaze and shook her head slowly. "I'm mentally preparing myself to deal with all the messes I'll be cleaning up once I have this little one," she said as she pointed to her belly.

Delia rolled her eyes. "Don't be ridiculous. You work with kids all day long," she said in reference to Ginger's job as a speech therapist at the elementary school. "Plus, once you have them, you laugh about the mess. Like me," she offered with a chuckle.

Their waiter approached. "Any refills?"

"Yes please," Ginger replied quickly, holding up her empty glass of water.

Delia shook her head, while Violet figured she could use one more glass of wine herself and slid hers to the end of the table. Their waiter filled Ginger's water and took Violet's glass before threading his way through the tables to the bar. Diamond Creek Brewery was crowded as usual. The low hum of conversation surrounded them.

Ginger looked back to Delia. "I suppose the mess is good for a laugh. I love working with kids, so I hope it's as much fun to be a mom. What about you?" she asked, her gaze swinging to Violet.

One thing Violet had come to learn about being thirty was most people had no qualms about asking about kids, whether you were with someone or not. She was used to the question, so she had a practiced answer. "That decision was made for me after I had leukemia. The chemo did a number on my eggs, so I got to get over the whole obsession about it sooner than most," she offered with a slight smile.

Her explanation left out was how devastating it had been to learn she didn't have the luxury of a choice. She didn't know if it was because she'd recovered from a major childhood illness, but she'd generally been a realist and tending toward sarcastic about life. It was hard not be a realist when a chunk of your childhood was spent in the sterile environment of medical settings while your parents hovered around with worry glimmering in their eyes at all times. It shaped a slightly bleak outlook.

Oddly, the way she used to be about romance had been a bit of a rebellion against that side of herself. She'd chased after the love of her life, a mystical creation that she thought she found. Reality gave her a vicious slap with that, and she'd done a lot of work to stay realistic about what she could have in life. Her last conversation with her mother came to mind—the point that she didn't like it when they worried over her, that she put up boundaries to keep people out. She had, and she'd thought she'd done so for good reason. After her engagement ended, she'd done her best to pull the frayed edges of herself together, yet she hadn't projected ahead how that might look. She wondered what to do now...and if she could find the courage to let herself hope for something.

Violet glanced between Ginger and Delia who'd both gone quiet. "Oh, don't worry. I've known for years. I'm okay with it," she offered, unsure how to interpret their expressions.

Their waiter arrived and delivered her glass of wine. Violet promptly took a gulp, reasoning she'd walked here, so if she got a little tipsy it didn't matter. Delia looked over at her, and Violet felt as if she could see right through her. It was nice getting to know more friends here. She had a few from work, but she'd spent so much of her first year here behaving a bit like a tourist who happened to have a job that she hadn't taken the time to find her tribe. That said, Delia's perceptiveness was a bit disconcerting.

"I suppose you kind of had to find a way to be okay with it," Delia finally said.

Violet sensed Delia had more thoughts on it and suddenly found herself wanting some serious girl talk. Her closest friend from New York was, well, in New York. Between their conflicting work schedules and the four-hour time difference, chances to chat on the phone were few and far between. She looked between Ginger and Delia and decided to dive in. "Okay, on this topic, I have a serious question."

Ginger narrowed her eyes. "Give it to us. We're great at advice," she said, so seriously Violet couldn't help but laugh.

Delia laughed with her, leading Ginger to glance between them. "What's so funny?"

"You," was all Delia had to say.

The moment gave Violet just enough bravado to lay it out. "I didn't find out I couldn't have kids until I was engaged. The shitty part was it was a no-go for my fiancée, so that was that." She paused to take a swallow of wine.

"Asshole," Ginger interjected.

Violet almost spit out her wine. Ginger's protectiveness was so fierce it was funny at times. "Maybe so, but once I got over it, I figured it was for the best. Anyway, to make a long story really short, I decided I'd rather be independent and didn't really want to worry about romance."

"Oh there's more to the story than that," Ginger added.

Delia nudged her with an elbow. "Let her talk."

Violet shrugged. "There is more to the story. Let's just say I used to be a tad foolish and silly when it came to romance. My break-up kind of woke me up, so I thought it would be best to be more level-headed."

Delia nodded slowly, her gaze assessing. "Romance isn't really level-headed for anyone," she observed, to which Ginger nodded emphatically.

"I might agree, but I get your thinking. You might think I'm lucky in love with Cam, and I suppose I am, but that was after my first husband treated cheating like a sport. Delia gets it too," Ginger said with a glance to her side at Delia.

Violet was naturally curious, but didn't want to pry. Delia saved her and said, "Oh, I get it. Nick's bio-dad took off the second he heard I was pregnant. I barely heard from him for years."

Violet was confused. "Wait, I thought Garrett…?"

"Was Nick's father?" Delia finished for her with a smile. At Violet's nod, she continued.

"He adopted Nick after Nick's bio-father died in a car accident. He's Nick's father in every sense that matters. Anyway, my point is just because you have a shitty experience with one man doesn't mean it'll always be that way. You might not believe it, but before I met Garrett, I was dead-set I'd never date again. Aside from not wanting to bother, I was crazy busy as a single mother. Then…" She shrugged and her cheeks flushed.

Violet glanced between them and almost burst into tears. After everything fell apart with Ted, she'd shored herself up behind strong walls. She'd been so happy to move to Alaska. Aside from her childhood dreams of coming here, it had also represented a fresh start for her, one where not everyone in her world viewed her through the lens of child-hood cancer survivor and dumpee. "Okay, guess I'm not the only one with a few battle scars. So, see all this was going just fine. I love being here in Diamond Creek, I love being in-dependent, and I really think I'm okay about my useless eggs." She paused for a breath, her cheeks flushing about what she wanted to ask next.

"It's Sawyer, isn't it?" Ginger asked, a subtle gleam in her eyes.

Delia elbowed her again. "I swear, it's a good thing you're so loyal and protective. Otherwise, you'd drive us all crazy."

Ginger swung to her, her eyes flashing. "How come?"

"You're pushy, and you bulldoze right into sometimes touchy topics," Delia answered quickly. "I still love you to pieces, but take it easy on Violet."

Violet burst out laughing. No matter what, Ginger lightened the mood, that was for certain. After she caught her breath, she forged ahead. "Yes, it's Sawyer. Honestly, I thought I was totally over the guy thing. Here and there, I'd feel a little zing, but never enough to care. With Sawyer, well…"

"Oh, we see what it's like with Sawyer," Ginger added with a wink.

Violet's cheeks got hot, and she took another swallow of wine. "What do you mean?"

"I was busy playing at practice the other day, but it was hard not to notice the chemistry between you two. Sawyer could barely keep his eyes off of you, and I'm pretty sure you were making out in the dugout. Just sayin'," Ginger said with a sly grin.

Violet could've used a fan to cool her face

about now, mortified to realize she and Sawyer were that obvious.

Delia elbowed Ginger again, but addressed Violet. "For what it's worth, you might as well know it's hard not to notice the way Sawyer looks at you. He's got that whole tall, dark and dangerous vibe going and then he turns all gooey-eyed when you're around."

Violet resisted the urge to squirm in her seat and clap. It was absurdly wonderful to hear that. She bit her lip before giving into the urge to grin like a foolish girl. "Okay, that's pretty good for my ego."

Ginger and Delia burst out laughing. Violet shook her head and sobered. "Here's the thing though. I can't let myself hope for too much. It's obvious he's a family kind of guy. That's not an option for me, and it's not fair to him if I don't say something about it before things get serious."

Ginger angled her head to the side, her gaze considering. "Well, I can't tell you what to do, but I don't think you should be worrying about that too much. For one, kids *are* an option for you. You just heard Garrett adopted Nick. It's not like you can't do the same thing, with or without Sawyer. I also don't think you should assume it would matter to him. Your ex was a jerk. Maybe it really did matter to him to have biological children, but if he really loved you, he would've tried to work through it together."

"I don't usually completely agree with Ginger, but I do now," Delia offered. "Don't cut yourself off from opportunities over what-ifs. I might not know Sawyer the way I know Garrett, but I don't think anyone in their family would be hung up on the bio kid thing. That's just not how they are. So don't make decisions based on assumptions. That never helps anyway."

Violet glanced between them. She was unprepared for the hard thump of her heart just now. Considering that the possibility of biological children might not be a deal breaker for Sawyer opened up vistas of hopes and dreams she'd long ago cast aside. It was a blessing and a curse for her. A blessing because maybe she could find the courage to be open to possibilities with him. A curse because she'd worked so hard to get a handle on her tendency to go all romantic and starry-eyed.

"I think you should give him a chance," Delia added.

Ginger nodded emphatically, her hair swinging back and forth as she did.

That silly hope shot up another flare inside

Violet's heart. She chewed her lip and traced the base of her wineglass on the table. "Okay. I guess I didn't really think about it like that."

Violet was quiet long enough that Delia spoke. "So was that your question?" she asked gently.

A rush of emotion rocked Violet. She took a deep breath and looked over into Delia's warm gaze. "No, it was more the impossible. What should I do?"

"Go for it!" Ginger said firmly.

Delia's assessing eyes search Violet's face, and yet again, Violet felt as if Delia could read her mind. "I think you wouldn't be asking if you didn't feel something for him. That tells you a lot," she finally said.

The knot of anxiety and tension inside Violet's chest kept tightening for different reasons. Sawyer was coming to represent far too much in her mind and heart. A glimmer of hope that perhaps she could let herself fall in love again, yet a risk so great she was afraid to take it.

At that moment, Ginger's eyes widened. "A change of subject is in order," she said quickly.

Violet's back was to the entrance, so she glanced over her shoulder to see Sawyer walking across the restaurant. She flushed straight through and her belly did a slow flip.

When she turned back, Ginger threw her a knowing look. "That's why I said you should go for it. You're about to go up in flames. That kind of chemistry only comes along once in a blue moon."

When Violet looked toward Delia, she grinned. "True. Anyway, let's talk about the weather," Delia said brightly.

Ginger said something about needing rain for her flower beds and elaborated on the state of her garden while Delia nodded along. Within seconds, Sawyer reached their booth. With a teasing smile, he greeted Delia and Ginger before looking at Violet. The second their eyes met, it was as if a bolt of lightning snapped the air around them. His gaze went from teasing to smoky, and he didn't say a word. Neither did she.

Ginger cleared her throat loudly enough Violet tore her eyes from Sawyer. With nothing more than a subtle gleam in her eyes, Ginger smiled at them. "Well, we'll get going now. Nice to see you, Sawyer." She glanced to Violet. "You'll be at practice Sunday afternoon, right?"

Violet managed to nod even though she felt like she was on fire. Delia said her goodbyes and then they left. The logical place for Sawyer to sit would be the opposite side of the booth from her. He looked over there and then down to her, promptly sliding into the seat beside her. She went from hot to melting. With a glance up in his eyes, her channel throbbed and raw need ripped through her.

CHAPTER 15

Sawyer stretched his arm across the back of the booth and forced himself to think about water heaters. He'd spent the last few hours helping Gage yank out an old one and replace it with a new one. He had to acknowledge he wasn't quite as steady on his leg as he liked to be, but he'd been able to add another pair of hands. Thinking about the details of properly getting the plumbing set was only marginally effective at quelling the lust surging through him.

Violet was just too damn beautiful with the layers of blue in her gorgeous eyes, her rosy cheeks and her mouth—her perfect mouth—lush and pink. All on their own, his fingers started sifting through the silky fall of her hair.

His body tightened in anticipation at her nearness, yet he also relaxed somewhat at finally being close to her again.

A waiter approached, at which point Sawyer realized he'd yet to even speak to Violet. He'd simply been staring at her.

"Can I get you anything?" the young man asked. He was all arms and legs with rumpled brown hair and brown eyes. Sawyer guessed him to be barely past twenty-one.

Violet glanced to him. "Have you eaten yet? Zach suggested the glazed salmon, which was amazing," she said, flashing a grin in Zach's direction.

Sawyer had wolfed down a snack at the lodge, but more food might be a good idea. "I'm not so hungry I need an actual meal. Whaddya have for appetizers?"

Zach started running down a list. The moment he mentioned crab-artichoke dip, Sawyer held a hand up. "That'll do. Bring a house draft with it, and I'm set."

With a nod, Zach picked up the dishes left behind by Ginger and Delia and headed toward the kitchen. Sawyer glanced to Violet. "Hey there," he said, very belatedly offering a greeting.

The flush on her cheeks deepened, sending

a jolt of lust straight to his groin. Damn. He did not want to be so helplessly whipped by her mere presence, he could hardly think straight. He wouldn't deny he wanted her fiercely, but he had some respect. If his instincts held sway over his mind, he'd throw her over his shoulder and find the first place he could to rip her clothes off and bury himself inside of her.

Water heaters, the weather, the tedious work of helping Gage lay the decking—those were all topics that might nudge his mind off of the lust cracking like a whip inside of him.

"Hey," Violet replied, a smile curling her lips. "Um, how have you been?"

He couldn't help but grin. His relentless efforts to keep his mind on something distracting were useless when she looked at him. He couldn't resist a flash of satisfaction at the desire he recognized in her eyes. There were many things he didn't know, but he knew what he felt when he was with her.

"Since I saw you this afternoon, I've been better than fine. I helped Gage and Don tear out an old water heater and replace it. How about you?"

She glanced at her watch and back to him. "You did that in less than three hours?"

"Yeah. Wasn't that hard, and there were

three of us. It was overkill actually, but Gage asked me to help, so I did," he said with a shrug.

Zach appeared at their booth, delivering Sawyer's beer and assuring him the dip and bread would be on its way momentarily before spinning away to another table. Violet sipped at her wine and leaned back. She'd changed out of the bright purple scrubs she'd been wearing at work earlier. She was dressed simply in jeans and a cotton shirt that had a scoop neck that dipped dangerously low, mostly because her generous breasts filled it out. His eyes dipped down, lingering on the curves, his body tightening in anticipation. He forced his eyes up and grinned when they collided with Violet's.

She took a gulp of her wine, setting the glass down and twirling the stem between her fingers. When she looked back at him, she was worrying her bottom lip with her teeth. She needed to not do that. Her straight white teeth denting her plump lip made him hard. Damn, damn, damn. He usually did not have this problem with women, even women he was interested in. With Violet, every sense was hyper focused on her, and his control, usually absolute, was tenuous.

He took a long pull from his beer and set it down, his fingers wandering along the downy skin at the back of her neck. He heard her breath hitch. Fuck it. He didn't care to try to be polite about this.

"Violet."

His voice came out rough, low and demanding.

Her eyes whipped up to his. He angled toward her, gripped her silky hair and fit his mouth over hers. She gasped, and he swept his tongue inside, pouring the need pounding through him into their kiss. A soft sound came from the back of her throat, spurring him on. One thing he'd come to love in the far too few times he'd kissed Violet was that once their mouths collided, she threw herself into it. Just now, she angled to him and threaded a hand in his hair. Their kiss went from hot to rough and wet.

A loud clatter nearby filtered into his awareness, and Sawyer broke free. He didn't pull away because he couldn't quite bear it just yet. His forehead fell to hers. Their rough breathing mingled, and he scrambled to gain some semblance of control. Violet made him crazy, and he didn't know what the hell to do with any of it. He knew one thing with certainty—he would have her again. Tonight.

* * *

VIOLET FELT as if she was moving through a fog —a hot, hazy fog of desire—as she walked beside Sawyer in the parking lot. She'd all but melted during the last hour with Sawyer close beside her in the booth, attuned to every flex of his muscled body. She'd been in bad enough shape before he kissed her and after that, well, she was simply a mess of need and longing. She was relieved she hadn't driven here because she'd gotten a bit tipsier than usual and, even better, it meant he was driving her home.

As they walked along, it suddenly occurred to her he had barely a hitch in his gait. She glanced up. "Looks like your leg is doing much better."

His eyes canted down, and her breath caught. In the shadowed light, his strong, chiseled features were sharpened, his eyes that deep, smoky gray that sent liquid need spinning through her veins. "It is," he replied simply. "Wasn't a major surgery, but annoying as hell beforehand."

At that, the palm resting on the dip in her

waist slid down to cup her bottom, and her channel throbbed. She'd given up arguing with herself in her mind—at least for now. Her brain had taken a backseat to her body, and all she could focus on was the hum of need simmering inside. When they reached his truck, he was quiet as he opened the door and made sure she was seated on the passenger side.

When he closed the door on the driver's side, the sounds filtering from the busy restaurant disappeared. It felt as if they were in their own cocoon. He started the truck and swiftly pulled out of the parking lot onto the road that led into downtown. Diamond Creek Brewery was situated towards the shoreline with a marshy field separating it from the ocean. Downtown Diamond Creek was only minutes away. He drove with one hand on the steering wheel and the other reached across the space between their seats, which at the moment felt like a chasm, and curled over her thigh. Her channel clenched, and she could feel the slippery heat between her legs. With her heart pounding wildly and her breath shallow, she tried to keep a handle on her body, but it was nearly pointless.

Within moments, he whipped his truck into the parking area beside her apartment. Puzzled at the bright light filling the area, she glanced up to realize one of the city trucks was parked in the street and a crew was working on the utility pole directly in front of the building. Before she had a chance to form a thought, there was a knock on Sawyer's window. He rolled it down, and they were greeted to a friendly smile from an older man. "You the ones who live upstairs?" he asked.

At Violet's nod, he explained, "The generator next door blew out these lines. They were testing it for some reason. Anyway, power's off here until we get it fixed. Should be back on within the hour."

Sawyer thanked the man, while Violet barely registered the details of what he'd said. All she heard was the power was out, which she didn't particularly care about, yet having an entire crew working on the utility pole right in front of her house didn't exactly fit with her mood. She turned toward Sawyer only to collide with his lips, which slammed against hers in a searing kiss. He threaded a hand in her hair and tugged her close, nearly devouring her mouth with his lips and tongue. She moaned into his mouth and almost sobbed when he broke free abruptly.

His hand slid between her thighs, and he

cupped her through her jeans. She swallowed, her hips reflexively arching into him. Oh. My. God. She was so close, she could almost come just from the feel of his palm barely rubbing over her clit through her jeans. The air inside the truck was snapping with electricity.

Violet jolted into motion, and flung her door open, all but running up the stairs to her apartment. She dropped her keys twice trying to unlock the door, by which point Sawyer had caught up with her. Oblivious to the lights illuminating them, they stumbled through the door. She heard the door slam shut behind her, and then Sawyer spun her around. In a flash, her back hit the door and his lips crashed to hers. Their kiss went from hot to hotter as their tongues tangled. His hard body crowded against hers, yet he couldn't get close enough for her. Fire roared through her.

She shoved her hands up under his shirt, greedily sliding over the hard muscled planes of his chest. With a muttered curse, he lifted his head, his eyes slamming to hers—hot and dark. The slick throb of her channel galvanized her. As he yanked her clothes off, she returned the favor. She lost her balance when she tried to kick her jeans free. He steadied her, his palm, warm and strong, curling around her hip. She leaned against the door and tried to catch her breath.

Which turned out to be impossible when she looked at him—his brown hair was rumpled from when she'd yanked his shirt off, his body was mouth-wateringly hard, and his smoky gray eyes were locked on her. While she was bare save her panties, bright purple cotton today, she suddenly realized he was much more efficient than she at removing clothing. While her fumbling with his clothes had only gotten her as far as his jeans ripped open and his chest bare. His bare chest was enough to stun her all on it own however.

He lifted a hand, tracing a single finger down along the side of her neck, down the center of her breastbone before tracing the sensitive underside of her breasts and circling up to roll a nipple between his thumb and forefinger. His touch struck sparks under the surface of her skin, leaving fire in its wake. Her nipples were so tight, they ached. She bit her lip to keep from crying out when he dipped his head, swirled his tongue around a nipple, and set to drive her wild alternating from one to the other.

If it hadn't been for the door at her back, she wouldn't have been able to stay upright.

With hot need pulsing through her, she shoved his jeans down enough to cup a palm over his cock—hot and hard. He murmured something against her skin and bit down on her nipple, sending a throb of pleasure straight to her channel. Restless and frantic, she shoved his briefs out of the way, sighing when his cock sprung free. Curling her fist around it, she stroked and started to shimmy down.

He held her still and stepped closer. In a flash, he shoved her panties down, lifting her against him as they fell to the floor. Her legs curled around his hips, and his mouth blazed a scorching trail of kisses down her neck while he stroked into her folds. He lifted his head. "Vi," he whispered roughly.

She dragged her eyes open and was immediately caught in his smoke-steel gaze. The lights from outside her window cast shadows in the darkened room. He dragged a finger back and forth, her hips rolling into his touch and a low moan escaping. "You're so wet," he murmured right as he slid a finger knuckle-deep inside of her.

She couldn't even form a word and simply stared at him when another finger joined the first and he set to stroking in and out of her. She was close, so damn close, to coming. He stopped suddenly, and her breath came out brokenly.

"Hang on," he said, his voice taut. "I need to feel you come."

She marveled at his strength as he adjusted her in his arms, holding her up with one while he fumbled in the pocket of the jeans hanging half-off his hips. She heard the tear of foil, and then he was rolling a condom on, the subtle pressure of his wrist brushing against her clit almost sending her over the edge.

"Sawyer."

His name was a plea, and he answered by whipping his head up. He adjusted her in his arms again, bringing her in line with the tip of his cock. Without a word, he held her eyes as he slowly rocked his hips into hers, nudging into her entrance. She arched into him, desperate for him to fill her, but he teased her—slowly nudging into her and pulling back, again and again and again. Pressure gathered, spinning tightly inside, as he pushed her closer and closer, yet held off from sinking fully inside.

Frantic, she curled her legs around his hips and arched against him. He sank to the hilt with a growl, his forehead falling to hers as his hips drummed into the cradle of hers. The contrasting heat of the cool door against her back and his hot body plastered to hers in front served to notch up the heat licking inside. She lost sense of everything but the delicious stretch of him filling her and the feel of his hard body surrounding her. Need lashed at her, tightening the pressure building. With every rock of his hips, she got closer and closer until he reached between them and pressed his thumb against her clit. The pressure spun loose, unraveling with a snap inside, as pleasure rocked her in waves. With a last drive into her, his head fell into the curve of her neck as he shuddered against her. The door rattled behind her, and she held on through the aftershocks.

Violet could feel his heart pounding against her skin, mirroring the percussive beat of hers. They remained still for several moments. The air whispered over her, and a shiver chased through her. Damp from her sweat, goose bumps rose on her skin. Sawyer lifted his head, his warm palm sliding down her arm. He opened his mouth to say something when the entry light flickered on. He grinned. "Perfect timing. I was about to say we should get in the shower, but then I remembered the power was out."

She looked at him, suddenly overcome with emotion. This intimacy she felt with him was almost too much. It wasn't just that they all but burst into flames when they were skin to skin. It was the comfort she felt with him. The part of her she'd worked so hard to make strong, independent, and free from the vagaries of silly hopes and dreams started to question the moment. She batted it away because she didn't want to listen. Not now.

Within the hour, she lay curled on her side with Sawyer spooned behind her. She was more relaxed than she'd been in, well, as long as she could remember. He was warm and strong and felt so damn good. She fell into a dreamless sleep, promising herself she would make sense of the madness another time.

CHAPTER 16

Sunlight fell across the bed in a wide path, its warmth and brightness tugging Sawyer out of sleep. The moment his senses came online, he tuned into Violet's soft, sleeping form curled against him. He was angled toward her, while one of her legs was draped over his and she was nestled against him, her palm resting on his chest. Nothing other than sleepy instinct driving him, his hand stroked up over the delectable curve of her bottom. Her skin was like silk. His body went from sleepy to alert, tightening at once as blood shot straight to his groin. He laughed to himself. Damn. He should be plenty satiated. After he'd taken her against the door, they'd managed to fall asleep, yet he'd woken during the night to find her hands mapping him. A stroke between her thighs where he found her slick with need had him rolling atop her and sinking inside.

Two explosive climaxes in one night were more than he'd had in years. Yet, all Violet had to do was exist and he wanted her so fiercely, he was calling upon unheard of reserves to keep a grip. When his hand traveled up over the curve of her hip and into the dip of her waist, she shifted and mumbled something. Glancing down, he saw her eyes blink open. His breath caught in his throat, and he swallowed against the tightness in his chest. She was flat gorgeous when she was sleepy and rumpled. Her cheeks were rosy, her blue eyes bright in the sunlight, and her dark hair mussed.

Her eyes landed on him and widened slightly. She was quiet for a moment before pushing herself up on an elbow, pulling the sheet up with her. "Good morning," she said, her voice raspy from sleep.

Holy hell. Even that turned him on. His cock hardened and he shifted his legs, so as not to make it obvious she turned him into a randy teenager inside. "Morning," he replied.

For a few beats, she was quiet, her eyes

coasting over him. He'd have given good money to see inside her mind. He didn't know what she was thinking, but he could sense the wheels in her brain spinning. After another moment, she spoke again. "Um, do you want some coffee?"

He was casting about for how to handle this morning with her. The last time he'd woken beside her, she'd quickly gone distant, albeit subtly and politely. He sensed the same thing happening again. It didn't help that he was on unfamiliar territory here. He'd spent much of his career as a Navy SEAL heading into dangerous situations where all he had on his side were his own well-honed tactical skills and the ability to handle some of the most challenging circumstances possible. Yet, he'd never faced the vagaries of an overwhelming attraction and the silken threads of intimacy binding him closer and closer to Violet. Oh, he'd known his initial attraction to Violet ran deeper than usual. What now felt like eons ago and was really no more than a month, he hadn't even known if he'd be around, so it hadn't worried him to follow the pull he felt toward her.

Now with his decision made to stay here, that added a layer of complication. He didn't want this to be a passing thing with her. Yet, given her asshole ex who'd dumped her and what little she'd said about her infertility, he knew she had some baggage. He had plenty of his own, yet it had nothing to do with romance. Rather it was about the weight of a few rough missions and nothing he didn't think he could handle. He'd been lucky enough to have parents who loved and respected each other. Hell, his siblings were shining examples of love and commitment these days. What was unfamiliar for him was the internal uncertainty, the sense of losing control when he'd lived his life in a place of control, strength and power throughout his entire career.

As these thoughts tumbled through his mind, he reeled himself in and realized he hadn't answered Violet's question. "Coffee would be great," he said quickly.

She nodded and scrambled off the bed, taking the entire sheet with her. So much for keeping it from being glaringly obvious the effect she had on him. She glanced back, her cheeks turning rosy red the moment she saw him. He was bare-ass naked with his cock oblivious to his mental wishes. He grinned and shrugged. "Ignore me. Seems to be a morning thing when it comes to you," he said with a chuckle.

He was heartened when she laughed, although she didn't return the sheet. She dragged on a t-shirt and sweatpants and scurried out of the bedroom, leaving the discarded sheet in a rumple on the floor. "I'll start the coffee," she called over her shoulder.

"Mind if I shower?" he asked as he stood.

At her muffled yes, he strode to the bathroom. A cold shower would shock his hard-on into submission. Moments later, he climbed out and found his clothes folded in a tidy pile on the sink counter. The smell of coffee filtered into the bathroom.

Once he was dressed, he walked into the living room and glanced toward the kitchen. Violet was dressed and snapping a lid on a to-go cup. She spun to face him. "All ready for you to take with you," she said brightly.

Sawyer wrestled with a flash of hurt. He didn't like how easy it seemed for her to wall him off like this. He stared at her, contemplating what to say. He wanted to push and demand she relax and let him stay and have coffee with her. Yet, he sensed that would only create more resistance from her. He needed to let her retreat, while he figured out what to do next. So, he walked to her. He curled his hand around the coffee cup, lacing his fingers through hers as he did. He was gratified to see her pulse fluttering along the column of her throat. Her cheeks went rosy again, and she bit her lip. He might be willing to let her create a bit of space, but he wasn't passing up the chance to kiss her again.

He dipped his head, pausing just before his lips met hers. "Have a good day, Violet."

Her breath went short, rising and falling rapidly. When she spoke, her lips moved against his. "You too."

At that, he closed the fraction of distance between them and kissed her—just once. He only allowed himself one glide of his tongue against hers. Any more and he might not be able to stop.

* * *

THE SUN WAS high in the sky and wispy clouds drifted on the breeze as Violet walked to the baseball field behind the high school. She'd spent most of the morning leading up to base-ball practice this afternoon obsessing over whether or not Sawyer would be here. Truth be told, Sawyer had been permanently lodged in her thoughts since she'd woken up beside him yesterday morning. She'd been restless and tied in knots inside over how much she wanted to cast all of her reservations aside. Her clear-thinking self had lost its voice, stamped out by her whimsical, foolish heart insisting she believe in the depth of the connection she felt with Sawyer. She couldn't think clearly about anything.

Every time she tried to tell herself to be rational, she started thinking about how it felt to be with him—a searing, burning, yearning connection that stitched her tighter and tighter to him every time she was around him. The feeling was exhilarating and terrifying at once. In the muddle of her head and heart, it was easiest to try to keep some distance. She'd busied herself with errands and cleaning yesterday, and ended up feeling lonely when she watched a movie by herself at the end of the evening. She'd woken this morning, swinging between the giddy wish to see him today and anxiety about how foolish she was.

She turned the corner around the building, voices carrying across the field to her. Ginger was tossing a ball to Nick who was practicing his swing. Garrett and Delia were standing nearby talking with Gage and Marley, while Cam was not far away laughing with Eli and Jessa. Sawyer was nowhere in sight, and she was instantly disappointed. So disappointed, it bordered on ridiculous. *You can't be this bad off. If you wanted to see him so badly, why'd you practically toss him out yesterday?* Her snide voice taunted her, and she sighed. She liked him, she really liked him, and she wanted to see him. All the more reason to get a handle on her feelings.

She reminded herself she'd been perfectly content the last few years. She'd accepted the reality of her life and committed herself to being independent. Moving to Diamond Creek had been one of the best decisions she'd made. It had been the change she needed to shake free of the tendency to hew to the careful habits she'd carried on from her childhood. Her mother's words rang in her mind—her gentle point that Violet created distance. She shook the thought away. Maybe her mother had a point, but it didn't change reality—she'd been slapped so hard by reality after she learned about her infertility, she wasn't inclined to let her tendency to tumble into things run her choices again.

Good. It was probably best Sawyer wasn't here. She'd enjoy baseball practice more without being distracted by his relentlessly distracting presence. She walked through the gate into the field and waved when Ginger looked over. Within moments, Ginger had assigned Nick to pitch to Violet, while Ginger raced around corralling everyone together. Other team members trickled in and within the next few minutes, they'd been sorted into 'teams' for practice. Ginger assigned Violet to first-base and ignored her when Violet tried to insist she wasn't ready.

"Only one way to get ready!" Ginger called as she jogged to second base to take her position.

Within the hour, Violet managed to catch two balls and miss two others. She also successfully batted and made it to second base, making it to home when the next batter sent a ball far into the outfield. Once she was playing, it was just plain fun. She forgot about being self-conscious and forgot about whether she was any good. While she was waiting on third base for her next chance to make it home, a subtle motion caught her eye. She glanced over to see Sawyer approaching the field. Her pulse instantly took off, and she flushed. Sweet hell. He was nowhere near her, but the effect of his presence was instantaneous.

It didn't help that he was just too delicious. As he got closer, his broad shoulders and subtle swagger sent a jolt of heat to her core. Damn. He was all kinds of tall, dark and sexy. As she was staring at him, she heard a high-pitched voice calling, "Saw!" and watched as he turned and knelt down to meet Holly with a hug, immediately lifting her up in his arms. Gage and Marley's daughter had arrived after practice started when Marley's mother dropped her off. All that hope Violet had been wrestling with fizzled instantly. One look at Sawyer with a too-cute-for-words two year old was like ice water being dumped on Violet's heart. Sawyer promptly began to swing Holly into the air, laughing with her as she giggled.

"Violet! Run!" Ginger hollered.

Startled, Violet looked back to the field and saw Gage dashing to first base as the ball he'd hit sailed over her head and into the outfield. Violet took off running and was relieved she made it to home base. Ginger was standing nearby, twirling a bat in her hands. She looked to Violet with a sly grin. "Little distracted, huh?"

Violet rolled her eyes and ignored the flush racing up her cheeks. For once, she wasn't blushing because she was hot and bothered from seeing Sawyer, no it was because she was flustered and rattled inside at seeing him with Holly. She was hot and cold at once, dread sitting like a lump in her stomach. At that moment, Sawyer stepped through the gate with Holly in his arms and started to head in their direction. Gage met him halfway and lifted Holly from his arms. Sawyer dropped a kiss on Holly's cheek and then walked over to where Violet and Ginger stood. "How's practice going?" he asked generally, his eyes flicking between them and lingering on her.

Violet swallowed and tried to make her body listen to her mind. It didn't. Her breath caught and flutters swirled in her belly. Her mouth went dry when she met his gaze—smoky gray flashing with silver. Her body instantly remembered the feel of him sinking into her in the dark hours of the night, her channel clenching with a slick throb at the visceral recollection. She'd never had this problem before—the problem of her body's responses so wildly beyond her control. Even when she'd been in love with Ted, or so she'd believed, she hadn't experienced this. Her attraction to Sawyer was on low burn when he wasn't around, while his presence was like a rush of air sending the flames of the fire licking hot and high. Meanwhile, she still felt half-sick with dread—all in all, her body was plain confused. There was what she instinctually wanted, and what she intellectually knew was a bad idea, a really bad idea.

Ginger glanced from Violet to Sawyer. With a gleam, she replied, "Great! Violet's made it to home base twice. She's officially a baseball player now." Ginger paused, her eyes scanning Sawyer. "When will you be ready to play? You're hardly limping."

Sawyer's eyes crinkled at the corners with his grin when he glanced back to Ginger. The respite from the heat of his gaze offered Violet a moment to gather herself. The second he spoke, a shiver raced through her at his gruff voice.

"You've got plenty of good players. What's the rush?" he countered.

Ginger put a hand on her hip and narrowed her eyes. "We're playing one of the teams from Kenai in two weeks, and they're really good. We need all the help we can get."

Sawyer shrugged. "Wish I could promise you I'd be playing, but my doctor would tell me that's stupid. I try not to be stupid. Maybe in a month or so."

"How about pitching?" Ginger asked swiftly.

He threw his head back with a laugh. "Not yet. I'll let you know when I'm ready."

Ginger wrinkled her nose and sighed. "Fine." Her eyes brightened. "I bet you'd say yes if I said you couldn't come to practices unless you were playing. It's rather obvious why you're here," she said with a wink.

Cam called Ginger's name, and she glanced between them. "Don't hide in the dugout," she said with a grin as she strolled off, spinning the bat in her hand.

Violet had only barely gotten her pulse under control when her eyes, greedy to soak up the sight of Sawyer, looked to him again. Off her pulse went, as if it was in a wild race. He met her gaze, his eyes darkening. The air around them hummed to life. Despite being surrounded by others with a cool breeze gusting across the field, it felt as if they were alone.

"You still think baseball is boring?" he asked, a gleam in his eyes.

She ignored the pounding of her heart and the heat sliding through her veins and ordered herself to behave like a normal person. A normal person would answer his question, instead of recalling the feel of his teeth grazing her nipple two nights ago. On the heels of a deep breath, she managed to form words. "Playing isn't boring. Jury's still out on watching," she said, calling upon her usual tendency toward sarcasm and forcefully trying to ignore the pangs in her heart elicited by witnessing him with Holly.

Sawyer's grin did that melty thing to her, where she felt all hot and unsettled inside. She ignored it, shoring herself up inside. This was lust, pure and simple. She'd get a handle on it as long as she kept that in mind. His eyes coasted over her, and she felt as if he was searching for something. It made her want to squirm. She was relieved when someone called out a greeting to him, and he glanced away to wave back. Garrett jogged over to them after being in the outfield for the last half hour.

Clapping Sawyer on the shoulder, Garrett flashed a grin between them. "Hey man. Didn't know you were stopping by today."

"Well with pretty much everyone I know here, figured it was worth a stop."

Garrett chuckled. "You still coming over for dinner tonight? Eli dropped off some fresh king salmon right before we came over here, so we'll grill it later."

Sawyer nodded. "Wouldn't miss it."

Garrett glanced to Violet. "You're welcome to come too if you'd like."

Violet shook her head quickly. "I appreciate it, but I can't make it," she said, completely lying. She had nothing else to do on a Sunday evening, but she needed to get some kind of grip. She desperately wanted to say yes because that meant more time with Sawyer, but the depth of her longing for him was startling. Mingled in with her longing was the aching pang of regret every time her mind flicked back to the way he looked holding Holly.

If Garrett picked up on anything, he didn't let on. He merely smiled and shrugged. "Another time then."

He headed off to help Nick gather equipment together as the practice wound down. Violet stood awkwardly beside Sawyer, worrying her bottom lip and wondering what to say. She was relieved for the activity around them as others meandered over to greet Sawyer. She took advantage of a moment to slip away when Jessa was chatting with him. She wasn't so cowardly she didn't say goodbye, but she made it quick. "Gotta go. I'll see you guys soon," she said with a little wave before jogging over to help Ginger carry a few bags out to the parking lot.

She needed to not be alone because if she was alone and Sawyer came over, she couldn't resist. Violet sensed Ginger picked up on something, but with others walking nearby, she stayed quiet. Violet loaded the bags into Ginger's car and jogged over to hers.

She was about to climb in when she heard her name. Glancing over her shoulder, she saw Sawyer approaching. *Dammit.* She didn't want to talk to him right now. She needed to get rational again. She gripped the top of the car door when he reached her, keeping it between them. He stopped on the other side, his gaze searching her face. "Everything okay?" he asked.

His tone was casual enough, but she sensed there was more to his question. Her mind flashed back to the recollection of him laughing as he swung Holly in the air. A sense of panic rose within, her chest knotting with anxiety and worry. Then, she went and blurted out the truth before her brain had a chance to interrupt.

"I can't have children. Ever."

His eyes widened, confusion swirling in his gaze.

Well, she'd gone there. Like a fool. So, she'd

better make sense of it. "I thought you should know. It's only fair."

Something flickered in his eyes, but she didn't know how to read it. His attention was like a laser, and it made her want to look away. "Fair?" he finally asked.

"Maybe it's crazy, but even though we're just...well, I don't know what we're doing. Anyway, it seems like most people would want to know what they could potentially be getting into if things got serious. I'm not saying we are, just that if it were even a remote possibility. I don't know if you think about things like that, but if you do, now you know. I, uh, well, it kinda messed up another relationship I had. The chemo that killed my leukemia also killed my eggs. So there." Her words had come out in a rush, which annoyed her to no end. She liked to consider herself strong and together. She usually was. Sawyer's appearance in her life had quickly disabused her of the silly notion that she was well over any possible weakness for men. Perhaps, she was, yet Sawyer was excluded from anything of the norm for her.

He watched her for a moment, his gaze softening. As if she wasn't already a mess inside, she'd just blurted out something really personal that could be interpreted to mean she thought they were getting serious when they'd only had two nights together. She felt like a kite in the wind—buffeted by her emotions, the depth of her attraction to Sawyer, and lingering remnants of the sense of loss she felt whenever she thought about her infertility.

He curled a hand over the edge of her car door and started to pull it open further. She clung to it tightly, keeping it as a barrier in front of her. He didn't wrestle it loose, but kept his hand there and looked at her intently. "Well, that's a bunch of bullshit," he said quietly, a thread of anger in his tone.

Confused and anxious, she asked, "Huh?"

"That something like that would mess up a relationship. Why should it matter? I mean, if you love someone, you love them," he explained. "I'm guessing it was hard to learn you couldn't get pregnant, but it's not like there aren't other options. Plenty of people adopt. Plenty of people don't have kids and are damn happy about it."

Violet stared at him, so many emotions circling inside she could hardly focus. The sense of relief that washed through her was immense. These were all the things she thought when Ted unceremoniously announced he couldn't consider marrying her if children were out of the question. At the time, she'd been scrambling to shore up her own emotions about her infertility, so she hadn't had it in her to think about adoption. In the two years since, she'd thought about it plenty. She didn't particularly want to raise a child alone, and she absolutely knew she didn't want to go through the pain of falling for someone only to have them walk again. So, she'd moved on and let go of those dreams. A rush of emotion welled, and hot tears pressed at the back of her eyes.

Sawyer angled his head to the side. "Are you okay?"

She swallowed and took a gulp of air, gripping the door so tightly her knuckles went white. After another deep breath, she managed to beat back her tears. He would think she was ridiculous if she started crying on top of everything else right now. She finally managed to nod and speak. "Yeah. I'm fine." Another deep breath. "I didn't mean to dump that on you there. I also didn't mean to make it sound like I thought things were more than they are with us. After what happened before, I..." Her words trailed off when he shook his head.

"Stop worrying about it. I get why you might want to say something. *If* we were serious," he said with a subtle gleam in his eyes.

She stared back at him, wondering what the little gleam in his eyes meant. *Don't you dare start hoping this can go somewhere.* She practically ordered herself to stop being hopeful. Because she had to. That gleam in his eyes certainly didn't mean she and Sawyer were going anywhere, she hastened to reason with herself. It most definitely didn't mean he was okay with the never having biological children option. *But he said people could adopt.*

Rising through the emotional cacophony inside of her was a tiny shout of joy. She wasn't supposed to get this excited. She wasn't supposed to get excited about anything resembling romance. Oh. My. God. Infertility might not be a deal breaker for him. This massive disappointment for her might not have to loom like a dark shadow in her mind. That was her hopeful voice, her silly romantic side that she'd tried so hard to quash. Oh God. This was bad for her. It didn't matter how hard she tried to be rational, she was so prone to full on tumbling into fantasyland over Sawyer. *Calm, stay calm.*

As she had a rational chat with herself, another part of her was yearning to say more, to ask him how he felt about what she'd just dumped on him. Her mind flashed again to the way Sawyer looked when he was holding Holly. She couldn't do this. She just couldn't be this stupid again. She met his eyes, clinging to the parts of herself that held her together after she learned about her infertility and her engagement blew up.

"I have to go," she said suddenly.

She started to climb into the driver's seat and pull the door closed. Sawyer tightened his grip on the door. "Wait a minute. Can we…?"

She shook her head, cutting right into what he was asking, as she fought to keep from crying. "No, we can't talk more. There's no point. If it wasn't obvious before, it should be now. I saw you with Holly out there. You deserve to have a chance for kids, and that's not an option with me. It doesn't really matter if we're serious or not. I won't be responsible for taking a chance like that away from anyone."

His eyes widened, her words startling him enough that he loosened his grip on the door. She didn't wait and yanked it shut. Within seconds, she started her car and backed up. As she drove away, she couldn't keep from looking in the rear view mirror. Sawyer stood right where she'd left him, beside the now empty parking spot, his gaze turned to the back of her car. A single tear rolled down her cheek, and she swiped it away quickly, only to have another follow. She forced herself to breathe slowly and beat back the ache in her heart.

Later that night, she kicked the blanket off of her legs and stood to return her plate to the sink. She'd had the kind of evening she'd usually enjoy. She'd watched a movie, chatted with her parents and made spaghetti. Yet, she'd spent most of the night trying not to dissolve into tears. She set her plate in the sink, the clatter of the silverware against the stainless steel loud in her quiet apartment. She sat down at the kitchen table with a sigh.

This ache in her heart and knot of tension in her stomach were visceral reminders of why she'd tried so damn hard to root this part of her out. Maybe Sawyer really was okay with the fact she couldn't have kids, but this thing, whatever she had going on with him, only illuminated a painful truth for her. The regret she'd thought long gone over that was still there. It was hard to think about falling in love and everything that went with it when she knew she couldn't have something she wanted deeply. She loved kids and loved the way they knit families together. Intellectually, she considered adoption a wonderful thing, but the doubts she held about her own capacity as a woman loomed large. It shouldn't matter that she couldn't conceive, but irrationally it did. She could hardly stand the idea of boxing Sawyer into losing the chance to have his own children. She lay in bed later, trying to tell herself she'd done the right thing. She had to break this off, or else she'd walk right into another broken heart.

CHAPTER 17

Sawyer knocked on the door to Garrett and Delia's house and stepped inside. "Hey there!" he called from the entrance.

"Hey bro, come on back," Garrett called in return.

Sawyer strolled past the stairs and under the archway leading into the living room and kitchen area toward the back. Their home was situated on a bluff overlooking Kachemak Bay. The living room had floor to ceiling windows, ensuring bright light year-round and offering a spectacular view of the water and the mountains rising tall on the far side. Garrett was seated at a round table over by the kitchen, his eyes scanning something on his laptop screen. A screeching call drew Sawyer's eyes to the windows, and he watched as an eagle took flight from a piece of driftwood on the beach, a raven hot on its tail. The raven was entirely oblivious to the eagle's massive size compared to its own and chased after the eagle, swooping and cawing. Sawyer chuckled as he watched, the eagle finally gliding into a cluster of trees atop the bluff. Sheer annoyance was effective on the raven's part as the raven turned and flew back to land on the very piece of driftwood where the eagle had been stationed.

It was midday with the sun glittering on the surface of the bay and the water ruffled by the wind. Between his various siblings moving here over the last few years, it felt as if they were all circling back to where they'd started, given they'd all been born here in Diamond Creek. Since Gage moved here, Sawyer had spent several of his breaks between missions here and didn't question he loved the area. Yet, his life was shifting gears in a major way. Years of being on active duty as a Navy SEAL was a far cry from how his life might shake out here. The breathtaking beauty was a definite bonus. He turned away from the windows and walked over to sit down across from Garrett. A curved counter divided the kitchen from the living room with a table tucked in by the windows.

Garrett clicked something on his laptop and quickly closed it, his sharp blue gaze landing on Sawyer. "Coffee?" he asked.

"If you have it. No need to make some for me."

Garrett winked and stood. "Always have it around. You know me. I might've slowed down a bit, but I still love coffee."

He stepped to the counter and poured two cups of coffee, setting one in front of Sawyer as he sat down again. He nodded toward the center of the table. "Cream and sugar if you need any."

"Nah. You know me. Like my coffee black." Sawyer took a swallow and sighed as he set the cup down. "Damn good coffee."

Garrett flashed another grin. "Delia spoils me. She made this before she left for work. I can make a decent pot of coffee, but I swear she adds something she won't tell me about. Hers is always better."

Sawyer chuckled. "Well, she is a chef."

"Yeah, but coffee has nothing to do with cooking. Not complaining though. I love it. So what's up at the lodge today? Gage called me yesterday about helping you guys with the business end of adding on backcountry hikes.

He's all about making sure the liability forms are lock-tight. What's up?"

"Oh, now that I'm here, he said he's been thinking on adding backcountry hikes and what-not. Says most of the local places are so booked, sometimes visitors miss out."

Sawyer forced himself to stay on topic. He'd been doing double-time to stay rational inside ever since Violet essentially dumped him after baseball practice. Somehow, based on nothing factual, he was determined to believe he still had a shot with her. As annoyed as he'd been with his family for nosing into his love life, he was now fighting the urge to dump his entire problem in Garrett's lap and get some advice.

Garrett nodded. "True. It's nuts here in the summer. Eli can barely keep up. Gage sends people to him, along with the Winters' brothers, but they're just as busy. I think it's a great idea. I'll draw up the legal details and you two can run with it. How you feeling about staying here?"

Sawyer took another sip of coffee and looked over at Garrett. "All in all, pretty good. It's the best decision for me right now." His mind flashed to Violet. He wanted to knock through the walls she was putting up. He'd texted a few times, and while it wouldn't be fair to say she was ignoring him, she was definitely keeping her distance. Her responses were polite, but distant. She simply wasn't giving him any openings to talk again.

Garrett eyed Sawyer and leaned back in his chair, his gaze coasting over him. Garrett was disconcertingly perceptive. His life now was a far cry from what it had been a few years ago. He'd been the hottest corporate lawyer in Seattle and lived to work. Sawyer had admired Garrett's brilliance and drive, yet Garrett had carried a driven, weary air in those days. The sly, funny older brother who loved to tease had taken a backseat to a life of work and more work. Sawyer had initially been surprised when he heard Garrett had up and moved to Diamond Creek, yet after he saw Garrett with Delia, he knew exactly why. Her warmth and generally kind nature softened Garrett's sharp edges. She also had steel hidden inside because she didn't hesitate to call Garrett out on anything. Together, they were perfect for each other.

Garrett had also embraced fatherhood in a way Sawyer hadn't expected. Garrett was more involved in Nick's extracurricular activities than Delia since he had more flexibility to his work schedule. While Delia was largely her own boss as the manager of the lodge restaurant and the reception and housekeeping, the job required her to be around for certain busy times. Garrett ran his own show completely with his law practice here in Alaska and a pared down office in Seattle for the few corporate cases he still handled. He could set his own schedule and happily did. He helped coach for every sport Nick played, which as far as Sawyer could tell was every sport possible.

This train of thought led Sawyer right back to Violet. Pretty much everything did lately. Before he could ask the question forming in his mind, Garrett interrupted his thoughts. "Seems like the best decision to me. What's up with Violet?" he asked.

Sawyer ran a hand through his hair. "She pretty much broke things off with me," he said bluntly.

Garrett's gaze sobered immediately. "Damn. What the hell happened?"

Sawyer took another swallow of his coffee and traced along the curve of the mug handle after he set it down. Part of him wanted to make light of it. That was his usual manner of dealing with things like this. He'd readily admit he was known as a flirt and a tease when it came to women, yet life on the move as a Navy SEAL hadn't offered the time, or the commitment, to focus on romance. Violet unsettled him, in part because almost from the start she'd thrown him off balance. There was that and what she'd laid on him the other day. She couldn't have kids, and it was obvious it bothered her. He wanted to storm over to find her and tell her it didn't matter. Yet, he didn't know if he could think clearly when it came to her. All he knew was he wanted her like he'd never wanted any woman in his life, and he could hardly stand it to have her try to box him out of her life.

"You okay?" Garrett asked.

"Not really," Sawyer finally replied after mentally girding himself to get through this. "I can't believe I'm about to say any of this to you, so cut me some slack, okay?"

Garrett nodded quickly.

"So yeah. Violet. I like her. A lot. Problem is, I don't know what the hell I'm doing. When we're together, it's, well, it's fuckin' amazing. Then she gets all squirrelly. I have kind of a weird question to ask if you don't mind."

"Of course not. Now you have to ask," Garrett said with a slight smile.

"Has it ever bothered you that Nick isn't your biological son?"

"Absolutely not. Honestly, if you'd asked me before I met Delia what I thought about getting involved with a single mother, I'd have told you it was crazy. Just goes to show how life changes you. Nick was six when I met Delia. His father, who'd never been around to begin with, died about a year later. I hadn't pushed before that because it didn't seem right, but I wanted to adopt him sooner. It sucks like hell his father died, and if I could change that for Nick, I would. If there's one thing I've learned in the process, it's that being a dad has basically nothing to do with whose sperm helped make the baby. Seriously, I'd take a bullet for Nick. It's impossible for me to even consider him not my son now. I wish I'd been there when he was younger, but I can't do a damn thing about that part. So to answer your question—no way," Garrett said, so fiercely it hit Sawyer right in the chest.

Garrett had a sheen in his eyes, and he took a deep breath before taking a sip of his coffee. "Didn't mean to get so intense there," he said with a chuckle. "Anyway, I have to wonder what made you ask that."

"Violet can't have kids, not the biological

way at least. She threw that on me right before she dumped me. She said it messed things up in her last relationship. I said what I thought, that it shouldn't matter. But I hadn't ever really thought about it much, you know? Pisses me off some jerk dumped her over it, but I wondered if maybe I was missing something."

"Asshole," Garrett said softly.

"Tell me about it."

"Well, maybe I'm missing something, but I know you pretty damn well. If you want kids, it won't make a bit of difference in how much you love them if you adopt or not. How's Violet feel about it?"

"Not that she explained a whole lot, but I'd guess she has some baggage around it. She had childhood leukemia and said the chemo killed her eggs along with the cancer."

"No matter what, it sucks when you don't have a say in things like that. Bad enough she had to go through chemo when she was a kid." Garrett paused and drained his coffee before eyeing Sawyer again. "Well, doesn't matter what you tell me now, you're serious about Violet," he said firmly.

"Huh?" Sawyer's question came out reflexively, while his heart gave a hard kick, almost as if to get his attention.

"You wouldn't be asking me anything about this if you weren't." Garrett winked and stood up from the table to place his coffee mug in the sink. He turned back and leaned his hips against the counter. "So whaddya gonna do about it?"

"About what?"

"Violet, you dumbass."

Sawyer glared at him. "I'm not a dumbass," he muttered.

"Most of the time you're not. Look, all I'm saying is you've only ever asked me for advice about one woman. Violet."

Sawyer leaned back in his chair and sighed. "Good point. See that's my problem. I don't do this kind of thing. My life hasn't made much room for it. I don't know how to deal with this. At first, I thought we'd kinda get past the hot and cold thing she was doing, but then she unloaded the kid thing on me and said she didn't want to keep me from having that chance. How the hell do I convince her that doesn't matter to me?"

"Tell her," Garrett said.

Sawyer stared at him before cracking up. Once he caught his breath, he asked, "That's it?"

"Well, have you even tried that yet?" Garrett said, his tone exasperated.

Sawyer rolled his eyes. "I thought I said so, but then she didn't really give me much chance to talk." He paused and closed his eyes. When he opened them, Garrett's sympathetic gaze met his. "But then I thought maybe I should think about it a little. I figured since you adopted Nick, maybe you'd be able to confirm what I thought. And you did. I don't give a damn about the biological thing."

"Doesn't matter. Not to me. Won't to you. It's good you took a few days, but don't sit on it. Go tell her."

"That's it? Just tell her?" Sawyer countered.

"Dude, I used to be as clueless as you, but I've learned a thing or two in marriage. Actually talking about things sometimes helps."

"Fine. I'll try it. Anyway, didn't you need my help with something?" Sawyer asked, ready to move on from the topic. Violet was spending so much time lodged in his brain, he was restless for something to take his mind off of her.

"Oh yeah. Need some help setting up Nick's drum kit. Ready?"

"We're setting up a drum kit? Since when does Nick play drums?" Sawyer asked.

"Since he started taking lessons. I could probably do it myself, but an extra set of hands would help. Plus, it's a surprise, so I want it done today before he gets home. You're a hell of a lot more patient than I am with that kind of thing."

Sawyer couldn't help but laugh as he stood from the table and followed Garrett upstairs to one of the spare bedrooms. He'd stayed in this very room once when he was home on leave. The guest bed was gone and a stack of boxes sat in the middle of the room. Within minutes, they'd unboxed the kit. As Sawyer helped Garrett, who clearly didn't need his help, assemble the drums, he couldn't help but marvel at how thoroughly Garrett had thrown himself into the life of a father and husband. For a man whose entire life had once revolved almost exclusively around his corporate law career, it was a marked change. Yet, it was obvious Garrett was far happier than he'd been before.

Sawyer left not much later with Violet on his brain and determined to talk to her soon. He was done waiting.

CHAPTER 18

"You can come next week?" Violet asked, her phone tucked between her chin and shoulder as she tossed an empty box in the recycling bin under the sink.

"Is that too soon?" her mother asked in return.

"No, I'll have to rush a bit to get things lined out at work, but it should be fine."

"Oh good. I was worried, but your father said the price for the plane tickets is only good until midnight. We'll have a whole week there!"

Violet adjusted the burner under the pasta, which was at a rolling boil, and turned to walk to the windows. "It'll be great to see you, Mom.

Anything in particular you want to do while you're here?"

One thing she loved about her parents was they were easy visitors. They preferred to stay in a hotel, which freed her from having to worry about hosting them and keeping her small apartment tidy at the same time. They also tended to go off on their own. She enjoyed spending time with them and certainly didn't mind if she needed to plan their entire week, yet that's not how they traveled. In the year plus since she'd moved to Diamond Creek, they'd visited twice last summer and again over the winter. At the moment, she was relieved to have something to take her mind off the ache in her chest ever since she'd broken things off with Sawyer. A visit from her parents would at least keep her occupied.

"Oh don't worry about planning for us. We definitely want to go fishing this year since we never went last year. Other than that, we just want to see you, hon."

"I'll make some calls and get a charter scheduled for us. Okay?"

"You don't need to do that. I'm sure we can figure it out when we get there."

"Mom, did you forget how many tourists

are here this time of year? I'm hopeful, but everything might be booked up already. Let me see what I can do. If you can't get a hotel room booked, you're welcome to stay here."

"Oh hon. We'll find something. Stop worrying."

Violet almost laughed. Her mother, who'd majored in worrying after Violet was diagnosed with leukemia, was telling her not to worry. "Okay, I'll stop worrying as long as you promise to let me know if you can't find a hotel with any openings. Try Midnight Sun Lodges. That place is huge. You take care of that, and I'll book the charter. Okay?"

"Deal. I need to hop online and take care of our reservations. I'll text you with the details. Love you!"

"Love…" Violet realized she was talking to no one. She slipped her phone into her pocket and stared out the windows. It was late evening, the sun just now sliding down the sky. Boats dotted the bay as they made their way into Otter Cove Harbor. An eagle sat sentry on the street sign at the corner nearby. Sawyer came to mind…again. For days, she'd been rubbing thoughts about him like stones in her mind, wondering what to do and if she'd made a huge mistake. She was torn about wanting to throw every reservation into the wind and call him and tell him she'd been an idiot. Every time she was tempted, she recalled the way he looked holding little Holly.

She thought she'd done a better job of moving past what happened with Ted than she actually had. She found it nearly impossible to let herself risk another broken heart. A tiny voice inside kept reminding her Sawyer had said adoption was an option. Every time she heard that, her more rational side stepped in and pointed out he was speaking in hypotheticals, not personally. Her heart gave a squeeze, and she shied away from dwelling on it. She couldn't, or she'd drive herself crazy.

She gave her head a shake and spun back to check on the pasta. Another dinner by herself. A perfectly common occurrence in her life. Usually, she'd be looking forward to the simple dish of pasta with olive oil, tomatoes, basil and fresh mozzarella. Instead, the internal disquiet she couldn't seem to quell made her feel restless and out of sorts. She wished Sawyer were here. That itself seemed silly because it wasn't like they had an established relationship. Yet, every time she thought of him, her heart gave a hard kick, almost as if to tell her something.

A few minutes later, she curled up on the couch and nibbled on her food. She'd determined she would call Sawyer tomorrow. Not because she planned to talk to him about, well, *them*, but because she needed his help. She hadn't had the heart to tell her mother there was no way in hell there'd be any charters available to book on such short notice. It was even less likely there'd be a hotel room available anywhere in town. Diamond Creek might be on the small side, but its tourist industry was massive. Hotels booked out over six months in advance before summer. She figured Sawyer might be able to help with that. A small corner of her mind whispered that instead of looking for an excuse to call him, maybe she should stare down what she was so afraid of.

The following morning, she hurried to work. She was relieved to be busy enough that she didn't zone out over fantasies of Sawyer. She hated admitting it, but that's what she did with half of her spare time. Between heated fantasies and internal battles with herself about Sawyer, it was mentally exhausting unless she was occupied. Thank goodness her job offered that most of the time. She made sure to check with her supervisor about taking time off and was thankful for the thousandth time she had an understanding supervisor who generally supported what she needed as long as she took care of things on her end.

She zapped off a text to Sawyer as she wolfed down lunch from the cafeteria and immediately moved onto her afternoon schedule. She was finishing up for the day when there was a knock at her office door. Figuring it was a co-worker, she called out for whomever it was to come in. Busy entering notes, she didn't look up when the door opened.

"Hey Vi."

Sawyer's gruff voice sent a ripple through her. Why, oh why did everything about him have to be so damn sexy? Her pulse took off at a fast gallop and heat suffused her. He'd called her Vi a few times the other night, moments when they were, um, otherwise occupied. She bit her lip and tried to gather herself before tapping save and spinning in her chair.

Sawyer stood there, his brown hair mussed, his dreamy gray eyes locked on her, and his body, oh sweet hell, his body—every muscled inch of it making her mouth water. His faded jeans hugged his legs and his black t-shirt pulled tight across his sculpted chest. Seriously, it was ridiculous the effect he had on her.

After a few beats of quiet, with her heart pounding so hard she worried he could hear it, he spoke. "Marley said your parents are all set for a room at the lodge, and Eli said he had a cancellation on a trip next week. He'll hold it for them."

She swallowed. He just had to go and be nice on top of it all. She knew he must think she was half crazy by this point. "Thank you. Really."

He shrugged. "No need to thank me. You can thank Marley and Eli."

"I will. I can't believe the lodge wasn't booked. When my mom told me they were coming next week, she was crazy enough to think they'd find a room. I let her try, but she called first thing this morning and said they'd had no luck. I think she said they even called Last Frontier Lodge." She forced herself to stay on topic even though her heart felt like it was about to crack open.

Sawyer shrugged, but he didn't add anything. His silence only set her pulse to a faster beat. "Sawyer, I… Ugh," she said, annoyed with herself for flailing about like this. "I hope you don't think I was only calling because I needed a little help. I, uh… Well, I know I kind of dumped some heavy stuff on you. I didn't expect anything like this. Because, well, because after I found out I couldn't get pregnant and my engagement fell apart, I kind of decided relationships weren't worth the trouble. And I was okay with that. I really was. I'm not one of those women who thinks love is the end all be all. I like my independence. I didn't really think much about any of it until, well, until you."

She paused and looked over at him. *What the hell are you doing?!* She screamed at herself. *You weren't supposed to get into this again. Shut up, shut up.* Once she'd started talking, the ball of tension in her chest started to loosen and she couldn't seem stop the words from pouring out. She'd said *way* more than she intended though.

His eyes held hers, but she didn't know how to read his expression. After a moment, he cleared his throat. "Okay."

When that was all he said, her stomach started to churn, and doubts crowded her mind. She shouldn't have said anything. She'd gone too far and made it seem like there was more to this than there was. She abruptly realized she'd started twisting the end of her ponytail in her hand and dropped her hand to her lap, fighting the urge to fidget. "Okay. Um, I guess I got ahead of myself again." She forced herself to look away, staring at a small photo taped to the back of her counter—a photo of two ladybugs nestled into a leaf. She couldn't say why, but it invariably made her smile, so she kept it there to look at on long days. Right now, it didn't work. She worried her bottom lip between her teeth and tried to think of what to say next.

"Vi," Sawyer said, his voice low.

She glanced back to him and saw him stepping inside her office and closing the door. Oh no. Her pulse lunged again. She watched him carefully as he took a few steps and leaned his hips against the counter opposite her. His eyes searched hers, making her want to blink and turn away. But, dammit, she wasn't a coward, so she forced herself to hold his gaze.

"You didn't get ahead of yourself. I actually almost stormed over to your place last night to make you talk to me, but then Marley suggested maybe you needed a little breathing room. So…" he paused and smiled ruefully, "I was trying to do that. Look, I didn't show up in Diamond Creek looking for any kind of relationship. Hell, I didn't even know how long I'd be here. The last few months of my life have been crazy. Between getting injured, dealing with the first round of my recovery and then waiting until they were ready to take care of this last bit, well I wasn't thinking about much beyond that. I get the whole unexpected thing. It's not like I can see into the future, but ever since I decided I was staying here..." His words trailed off, and he shifted his shoulders. "I guess what I'm trying to say is I'd like to give us a shot. I'd like to say I know what I'm doing because, well, I'm that kind of guy. I usually know what I'm doing," he offered with a low chuckle, sending her belly into a tailspin of flutters. He continued, "...but my life hasn't offered many chances for anything other than casual relationships here and there. In a roundabout way, you didn't get ahead of yourself. At least not for me. Much as I'd like to rush you into this because..." He looked straight at her, catching her in his dark, hot gaze. He didn't need to explain because his eyes did it for her. The air snapped to life, as if jolted by the electricity crackling between them. "Here's the thing. Not that you're asking, but kids aren't a deal breaker for me. I figure you need to know that. Other than that, I'm putting the ball in your court. If you want more, I'm here. Okay?"

Violet stared at him, her mind and body in an all out battle inside. She could seriously use an off switch in her brain. With an act of sheer will, she ignored the chatter and pulled herself together. How the hell was she supposed to respond to this? The small hopeful voice inside of her that she'd worked so hard to shut up was running around screaming with joy. Kids weren't a deal breaker for him! The rest of her was stunned into silence and frozen. She was actually annoyed he wasn't forcing her hand. That would've made this all so much easier. But no. He was too damn confident. That was the thing. She'd always been turned off by pushy guys because it illuminated their weakness underneath. Sawyer had to go and be strong enough to tell her she had to come to him on her own terms. Warring with herself, she stood abruptly, her wheeled chair rolling and bumping into the counter behind her.

"I guess it has to be okay," she said, the prickly feeling inside notching up when his mouth curled at one corner.

"It doesn't have to be okay," he replied.

She chewed at her bottom lip and tried to corral the wild feelings coursing through her.

She was hot all over, nearly overcome with sudden longing for him, and furious with herself for being such a mess inside. When she glanced up and collided with his gaze again, she spun away and practically stalked to the door. "Okay. I guess I do need some time. I'll… I'll call you. Or something," she said, reaching to open the door, only to feel it slam shut the moment she started to pull it open.

Sawyer's palm lay flat against the door. He took another step and rested his other hand against the door, effectively caging her in between the door and his body, every hard, heated inch of it. Her breath caught, and she swallowed against the rush of longing that surged through her.

"Or this," he said right before his lips crashed to hers.

His kiss sent her up in flames. He nudged closer, plastering himself against her, and proceeded to drive her nearly mad with the hottest, deepest, most devouring kiss she'd ever experienced. She was close to collapse and almost melted into a puddle by the time he lifted his head. One more hot look from him, and he stepped back. "I'll be waiting," he said when she managed to straighten and push herself away from the door.

She closed the door behind him and sank into her chair, her entire body shuddering softly. She could feel the moisture between her thighs and shook her head slowly. Dear God. He'd rendered her nearly useless with a single kiss. Just one kiss.

CHAPTER 19

Sawyer walked down the stairs from the back hallway at the lodge into the restaurant kitchen. He'd temporarily relocated to the spare bedroom in Gage and Marley's quarters. He hadn't bothered to tell Violet, but the reason her parents had a room at the lodge was because he'd volunteered to give up his suite. Gage regularly kept one suite available for friends and family at all times, no matter how busy the lodge was. With the lodge in its third year of operation, they were booked year-round these days. Sawyer had known it was likely a lost cause for Violet's parents to find a place anywhere in town on such short notice. Once he spoke to Marley and Gage, they collectively agreed it was the only option.

He could also stay with Garrett and Delia, in addition to Jessa and Eli, but what few belongings he had were here, so it was easier to stay in the same place.

He pushed through the swinging door into the kitchen and aimed straight for the coffee in the corner, giving Delia a quick wave. Her blond hair was tied up and her apron was covered in flour. He knew she spent most of her morning baking, a fact for which he was incredibly grateful. She made cinnamon rolls to die for, and he was getting downright spoiled having them every day.

"Morning Sawyer!" Delia called across the kitchen. "Violet's parents checked in late last night according to Harry."

He poured a cup of coffee and walked over to the opposite side of the massive stainless steel table that ran the length of the kitchen. It had been almost four weeks since his surgery, and damn did it feel good to walk without pain. It had only taken two tiny arthroscopic incisions to make the pain go away. He hitched a hip on the table and savored a sip of Delia's coffee. "Garrett's right," he said with a grin.

"Tell me what Garrett's right about," Delia said with a smile as she rolled pastry.

"You make better coffee than him."

She laughed. "Ah. He thinks I'm doing something secret."

"Garrett likes to be the best at everything, so if he tells himself you're secretly adding something, he can trick himself into thinking he might be just as good at it if he knew what it was."

Delia nudged a hair out of her eyes with her elbow and set the rolling pin to the side before carefully cutting the pastry dough into strips. "True. Anyway, I was thinking we should invite Violet and her parents for some kind of dinner thing while they're visiting. What do you think?"

Sawyer's chest tightened. He wanted to see Violet, but he'd rather have her all to himself. He hadn't heard a peep from her since their conversation a few days ago with the exception of one text thanking him again for helping find her parents a place to stay. He'd seen her briefly at a baseball game, which he went to watch solely for the purpose of running into her, yet she'd barely said hello. He was torn inside. He was bound and determined he wasn't going to play his hand too soon. That would make his hand all the weaker. He could wait. He also sensed Violet needed the space. But hell, it was not easy giving it to her. He was thankful he had plenty to keep him busy. When Gage had said he could use the help around the lodge, he'd meant it and then some. There was always something to do. Delia cleared her throat, and he glanced over to her.

"I'm guessing you don't know about that dinner, huh?" she asked with a soft smile, her eyes curious.

She wouldn't push, and he knew that, which actually made it easier to talk with her. "It's a great idea. Her parents will be here anyway, so if you let me know when, I'll call her. I'm sure she'd love it."

"Perfect. I'm not manning the kitchen the night after tomorrow, so let's aim for that. You talk to her, and I'll round everyone else up." She paused to spin around and check something in the massive oven behind her. When she turned back, her perceptive blue gaze landed on him. She angled her head to the side and drummed her fingers on the table. "What *is* the status with you two anyway? I noticed you kind of played it cool at the baseball game the other night."

Little did she know it had taken all of his discipline not to toss Violet over his shoulder and carry her off the field after she'd hit her first home run. Their team won the game against Kenai, and Violet's cheeks had been rosy, her hair a wild tangle, and her body deliciously outlined in her black leggings and fitted t-shirt. Instead, he'd congratulated her in the muddle of friends before making his way back to his car. Ginger had cajoled him into agreeing to start practicing with them as long as he only pitched in practice until his doctor cleared him to run.

He gave himself a shake and looked over at Delia. "Hell if I know. Ball's in her court," he said with a shrug.

Delia returned to cutting strips of pastry dough. "Why's the ball in her court?"

"Because I don't know what the hell to do. I mentioned to Marley that I couldn't make heads or tails of how she felt. Marley suggested maybe I lay low and not get too pushy. So before you go thinking I'm being difficult, I'm following Marley's advice," he replied, a tad defensively.

Delia glanced up as she worked, a small smile on her face. "I didn't say anything was wrong with it. Just curious."

He took a long swallow of his coffee and set it down with a sigh. "What do you think I should do?" he asked.

She turned and grabbed a covered bowl out

of the refrigerator nearby. She began spreading some kind of filling on the strips of dough and rolling them up. Sawyer couldn't help but wonder what she was making, but he refrained from asking because he really wanted to know what Delia thought. In the few years she'd been with Garrett, Sawyer had come to know her as rational and warm when it came to advice. He was starting to get impatient when she finally spoke.

"I think maybe you might be doing too good of a job with playing it cool," she said.

"What do you mean?" He felt like an idiot here, and he hated it. His entire adult life had been about control, discipline and functioning incredibly well under high pressure. He felt like he was stumbling about blindly here.

"Did you happen to notice she followed you out to the parking lot after the game the other night?" Delia asked.

He almost choked on his coffee. "What?!"

Delia sighed and shook her head. "Uh, yeah. She actually ran after you. I was on my way already, so I saw the look on her face when she watched you driving away. She looked really bummed."

Sawyer realized his mouth had fallen open, and he snapped it shut. He pushed off the table and went to pour another cup of coffee. Returning, he ran a hand through his hair and sighed. "So I looked like an ass?"

"Oh no. That's not what I meant. Just that it seemed like she wanted to talk to you, but you bolted so fast, she didn't have a chance." She carefully placed the spirals of pastry she'd created onto a tray. "You know, I don't know you all that well yet, but I can guess you're used to being in control."

"Definitely," he added.

"Well, the thing is no one feels in control when it comes to relationships. From what I can gather, Violet might have some reasons for keeping her distance. You might have to go out of your way to make sure she doesn't misinterpret things."

Sawyer took a bracing gulp of coffee and glared at Delia. "Could you and Marley chat and make sure you're giving me consistent advice?"

Delia grinned. "Not so sure it's conflicting advice. There's giving someone space and then giving someone so much space, they might be confused you're not interested. You have to find the balance."

He nodded numbly, his brain practically mush from overthinking this thing with Violet.

What he hated the most was how much it mattered. He'd been doing his damnedest to convince himself he only wanted a chance to see where things went with her. But just hearing she'd tried to talk to him after the game nearly tore him in two. To think she might think he didn't care? Hell, he cared. He cared way too damn much.

He glanced over at Delia as she lifted the tray of pastries and turned to carefully slide them inside the oven. When she looked over her shoulder, he asked, "Did you suggest this whole dinner thing because you're matchmaking?"

"Maybe," she said with a sly grin.

"Maybe you should check with Marley if that's a good idea," he said with a roll of his eyes.

Between Becca and Jessa, he was accustomed to the women in his life having opinions about what he did. The unintended bonus to being out of the country for months at a time was his sisters generally let him be when he was around. He knew perfectly well that if Becca or Jessa had a clue about his feelings for Violet, they'd be all over him. Becca, the most opinionated of all of his siblings, was ensconced in her life with Aidan in Seattle. Jessa had been so busy since he'd been here, he'd barely seen her since his day of fishing and dinner with her, Eli and Ryan. Now he had two sisters-in-law to add to the mix of opinions. Thank God he loved them both.

Delia closed the oven and turned to face him, hands on her hips. "Maybe you should face your feelings and do something about it."

For the second time, he almost choked on his coffee. Delia could trick you into thinking she was nothing other than warm and kind when in fact she had steel in her spine and was one of the few people with the nerve to call Garrett out when needed, so he should've been prepared. He straightened and met her gaze head on. "Okay then. Maybe I will." He started to walk out and then turned back. "You know, you could've told me this before her parents were here. Now I've gotta navigate them too."

Delia chuckled. "Gage swears you function best under pressure. Deal with it."

At that, she spun away, calling Harry's name as she pushed through the swinging doors into the restaurant. Sawyer glanced at his watch and wondered where the hell Violet was.

CHAPTER 20

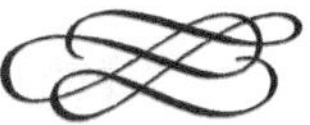

Violet pulled into a parking spot at Last Frontier Lodge and looked through the blurry view. It had been raining all day and hadn't let up. She watched a raindrop roll down the windshield in a wavy path until it disappeared at the bottom. Her well-planned schedule for while her parents were here had already gone sideways when the hospital begged her to come in today after the only other phlebotomist on staff got sick with a nasty stomach bug. Those occasionally ran like wildfire through town with tourists bringing all kinds of fun viruses with them. Normally, her supervisor would step in, but she was sick too. Violet was relieved it had turned out to be a rainy day, so her parents had elected to take the day to visit shops and galleries while she went to work.

She took a breath and let it out slowly. She was anxious about seeing Sawyer. She'd impulsively chased him to the parking lot after the baseball game the other night. With her nerves running on the fumes of adrenaline from the game, she'd decided to take the ball he'd tossed in her court and run with it. Only to find him driving away when she got there. She'd been determined to try to clean up the mess she'd made after their last talk after baseball practice. He'd been so polite and distant right after the game, she worried her wishy-washy behavior had driven him away. So, she'd come a little earlier than she was supposed to see her parents to try to talk to him. On the heels of another breath, she forced herself to move. The last thing she wanted was to delay so long that her parents were downstairs in the lodge before she found Sawyer.

She'd forgotten her raincoat at work when she left in a hurry. When she'd realized it, she figured she didn't have far to dash through the rain. Yet, she hadn't counted on the parking lot being so crowded and was parked about as far away as possible from the entrance. With another deep breath, she shoved the door open and slammed it shut behind her as she began to hurry through the parking lot. The wind gusted sideways, blowing the rain in sharp spikes against her cheeks. Putting her head down, she kept moving and didn't even see the delivery truck pulling out of the parking lot. She heard the hiss of the brakes just as she looked up into a face full of water. In less than a second, she was soaked from the large truck rolling through a puddle.

She stood stock still and sighed. This was her day, or rather her week or so. The driver was kind enough to roll down his window. "Sorry about that! Didn't see you running this way. You okay?"

She glanced up to find a jolly looking man with a wide smile and twinkling blue eyes in his weathered face. "I'm wet, but I'll be fine. Thanks for checking," she called out.

His smile stretched wider. "Go get inside where it's warm and dry then."

At that, he continued driving while she couldn't help but return his infectious smile. With water dripping from her hair and her wet clothes sticking to her, she made her way inside. She paused inside the entryway and dragged her sleeve across her face, a rather pointless effort to dry herself seeing as her sleeve was soaked too. She glanced around and was relieved to find no one immediately present. She figured she'd track down Delia or Marley and find a towel or two. It was midday, so there was a soft hum of voices coming from the restaurant. She didn't want to impose and overstep, but she certainly didn't want to tromp through the restaurant looking like this. With another glance down both hallways leading off of the reception area, she walked behind the desk and through the door that she knew led into the kitchen.

She didn't realize she was shivering until she stepped into the warm kitchen. Two line cooks were busy at the grill, while Delia's back was to her as she checked something in the massive oven against the far wall. Violet was suddenly self-conscious and started to turn away when Delia called a greeting.

"Hey Violet!"

Violet turned back. Before she could explain, Delia's eyes widened. "Oh no. You're soaked. I'm guessing that's why you came in this way." She gestured for Violet over to her. "Come on, you can shower and dry off in my office."

Violet hurried across the kitchen, water dripping with every step she took. "I'm sorry. I got splashed when a truck was pulling out of the parking lot."

Delia shook her head. "No need to apologize. Right here," she said as she opened a door at the back of the kitchen.

Violet walked through the door and looked around. Delia's office was small and cheery. She had a plant hanging in the window and a brightly colored rug on the floor between a desk and couch. Delia closed the door behind them and stepped past Violet through another door. "Oh good, I have clean towels in here," she said.

Violet peered into the room and discovered a tiny bathroom with a sink, toilet and corner shower. "Oh wow, what's a shower doing in here?"

Delia grinned. "Back when my mom ran the kitchen over thirty years ago, she had the Hamilton's install a shower because she got sick of my dad coming in off the slopes all dirty from whatever he was working on. Gage asked if I wanted it torn out, but someone uses it a few times every week, so we keep it." She paused, her eyes coasting over Violet. "You need dry clothes. I'll call up to Marley and have her bring something down. You're shorter than her, but otherwise you two are close enough in size that you can get by. Okay?"

"You don't need to do that. I'll just…"

Delia shook her head firmly. "I didn't mean to make it seem as if I was asking. I'm guessing you're here to see your parents, and you're soaked. Either you sit around in wet clothes for dinner, or you drive home in wet clothes to change. Both options are silly when Marley lives right upstairs. You hop in the shower, and I'll leave some clothes in the office and lock the door on my way out."

Violet, knowing determination when she saw it, acquiesced. "Okay, okay. Thanks. Really," she said. "It's been that kind of day, so a little help goes a long way."

Delia smiled warmly. "Anytime."

While Violet was absorbing how nice it felt to have made a new friend like Delia, Delia stepped out of the office and closed the door behind her. Violet took a deep breath and let it out. Her anxiety about talking to Sawyer was churning inside and getting worse because she felt like a drowned rat. This wasn't exactly the look she was going for. With another sigh— she'd been sighing a lot lately—she stepped into the bathroom. She tugged off the denim blouse she'd worn over a tank top, her skin pebbling in the chilly air, although she was immediately relieved to have the wet fabric off of her. Simply untying her shoes was a challenge. The laces were wet and tangled from her run through the rain. She leaned her hips against the wall and fiddled with them, swearing to herself.

She heard footsteps and then the door to the outer office opening and closing, figuring it must be Delia delivering her borrowed clothing. "Thanks Delia!" she called through the door.

She kicked off her second shoe and started to peel off her jeans, only to jump when the bathroom door opened. Sawyer stepped through. Startled, her mouth fell open and she stumbled back against the wall. He looked so damn good, it almost hurt—his worn black jeans molded to his muscled thighs, and his black t-shirt serving only to show off his mouth-watering chest and abs. He needed to stop wearing black. It took the whole tall, dark and sexy vibe too far. With his chocolate brown hair mussed and his flashing smoky silver eyes, it was all she could do to stand upright. Thank God for the wall holding her up.

His eyes collided with hers and then brazenly conducted a slow perusal of her. She flushed instantly. Her jeans were halfway down her hips with her bright purple panties visible. Her tank top, unintentionally matching purple cotton, stuck to her breasts. Without looking, she could feel her nipples standing at attention. She'd already been chilled, but then Sawyer showed up. If her nipples could talk, they'd squeal. Her belly fluttered and wet heat built between her thighs. This was not good. Not good at all. She'd been battling internally too much and held back from what she wanted, which was Sawyer. Quite specifically…Sawyer. Naked. Inside of her.

When his eyes made their way back up and landed on hers again, she swallowed. *Oh. My.* Okay, so maybe he still wanted her if the look in his eyes was any indication. He cleared his throat. "Delia called up for Marley to bring some clothes down." He paused and took a step closer. "Marley wasn't home." Another step. "I brought some down for you."

Another step, and he stood right in front of her. The air pulled taut and nearly snapped under the pressure of need shimmering around them. "I've been wanting to talk to you," he said.

She could hardly breathe, but managed to

nod. "Me too." Her words came out in a rough whisper.

"I don't want to talk right now though."

His eyes held a question. Raw need scored her. She nodded, answering his unspoken question. He lifted a hand and traced one of her nipples before rolling it between his thumb and forefinger. She moaned and her head hit the wall with a thud. The next few moments were a wild blur, as he suddenly swore and stepped back. With one swift motion, he yanked her tank top over her head. It fell to the floor, slapping against it. His need matched hers as he flung her bra off, while she tore his jeans open and pushed his briefs down over his hips. His cock sprang free, and she sighed at the feel of his hard, hot length in the grip of her hand. He didn't give her a moment to savor and shoved her jeans and panties down around her ankles, lifting her against him as he did. She kicked her legs free and curled them around his hips, crying out into his mouth when he took hers in a scorching kiss.

She could feel the tip of his cock at her entrance and nudged him with her heels. She needed him inside of her. Now. She needed it hard and fast. Suddenly a loud clatter from the kitchen startled her. She tore her lips free. "Oh my God. Someone might..."

"I locked the door. No one's coming in," he said swiftly, arching his hips just the slightest bit.

She bit her lip to keep from crying out. She met his eyes, and her heart gave a hard thump. When she was this close to him, she forgot everything else—all the worries crowding her mind, the doubts she'd carried from her past, all of it dissolved under the force of their connection. He held her gaze for a long moment, and then closed his eyes.

When he opened them again, his gaze was pained. "I can't believe it, but we have to put this on pause. Delia told me you were here, and all I was thinking about was seeing you. I didn't bring a condom with me."

He started to ease back. "I'll..."

"Oh you're not going anywhere," Violet said, tightening her legs around his hips. "I can't get pregnant, so birth control is pointless. I'm clean, and I trust you are too."

Her heart was pounding wildly, a percussive rhythm echoing through her entire body. Sawyer looked at her for a long moment before nodding. "I'm clean. Are you...?"

"I'm sure," she said, cutting him off.

She tried to yank him to her, but he held firm. "Vi, look at me."

She whipped her eyes to his and felt split open inside, as if he could see right into her heart.

"This isn't just about sex for me," he said gruffly.

She swallowed against the emotion knotting her chest and took a breath. "It's not for me either," she whispered.

He held her gaze for several more beats. Though not another a word passed between them, it felt as if they had an entire conversation. The tension she'd been holding inside eased. He stepped closer and let his forehead fall to hers. Adjusting her in his arms, he reached between them and stroked his fingers through her folds.

"You are so fucking wet," he murmured.

Impatient, she spurred him with her heels. On a low chuckle, he angled his hips and arched, moving his hand out of the way as he sank to the hilt. She started to cry out, and he caught her lips in a fierce kiss.

It had been too long since she'd been with him, wrestling with the force of her desire for him on so many levels. With his hips pounding into the cradle of hers, the delicious stretch of his cock filling her again and again, and the frantic beat of their hearts, her release was upon her almost instantly. The pleasure tightened to a wild peak and then burst loose, unraveling and whipping through her body. He caught her cries in his kiss, his own body going rigid before she felt his release pour into her. He slowly drew away from their kiss, catching her bottom lip in his teeth before dropping his head in the curve of her neck. She could feel his heart pounding against her skin. She'd gone from wet and cold from her inglorious drenching in the rain to steamy inside and out.

As Violet's pulse slowed gradually, she idly sifted a hand through Sawyer's hair. He lifted his head. The moment his eyes met hers, she felt raw and exposed—bare in more ways than one.

"I missed you," he said simply, his gravelly voice sending a shiver over her skin and reaching right inside and grabbing ahold of her heart.

She pushed back against the fear crowding her mind. "I missed you too. I, uh, tried to catch you after the game the other night, but…"

He smiled ruefully. "I took off a little too fast. Delia mentioned it to me. I guess I took the whole 'giving you some time' a little too far. Between the two of us, I'm guessing you've had more experience with relationships than me. I'm used to knowing what to do. With this…" he laughed softly, reaching up to brush a damp lock of hair off of forehead.

There was another loud clatter from the kitchen and a muffled curse. Violet glanced toward the wall adjoining the kitchen, as if she could somehow see what had happened. When she looked back to Sawyer, his smile nearly undid her when he'd already left her boneless. "My experience wasn't so helpful." She paused to adjust her hips because she was sliding down, only to slide further down the wall.

Sawyer, being nothing other than strong and solid, easily lifted her up in his arms. With a grin, he slowly stepped back, slipping out of her and setting her on the floor. "Let's get you in the shower. We can keep talking."

He reached into the tiny shower and turned the water on. In seconds, steam was filling the bathroom. He kicked off his jeans and tossed his t-shirt on the sink. She stepped under the hot water and sighed as the heat seeped through her. The interlude with Sawyer had thawed her, but she'd been drenched to the bone with cold rain. He climbed in beside her, and to say it was crowded might be an understatement. She turned in his arms and glanced up to find him waiting.

"You were saying?" he asked.

She dipped her head under the water and rinsed the soap off. "Um, we're talking here?"

He nodded. "Good a place as any."

"Okay, so my experience…right. Well, aside from getting engaged and then finding out I was infertile and getting dumped over it, my experience with relationships before that was a bit foolish," she said bluntly, figuring she'd just lay it out there.

"Foolish?" He arched a brow as he stepped back, creating a minuscule pocket of space between them as he grabbed the soap and quickly slid it over his arms and chest. Oh God. He was too much with every delectable, mouth-watering inch of his rock hard body slick with soap and water running over him. She glanced down to see the small scars from his surgery healed up. That leg had other scars, including a jagged one running along his outer thigh. Her heart clenched, but she didn't want to dwell on that now. He was strong and healthy and right here with her.

"Foolish because I was kind of silly and romantic. When you're sick like I was and people hover around you and worry and then you get better, well it does weird things sometimes. It made me hope for the best. For a while, I was afraid I might not get that chance. So I was ready to settle down the first chance I got. I'm still not sure I really loved Ted, but I sure thought I did. Anyway, that's what I mean by foolish."

Sawyer looked at her, his eyes flashing silver through the smoky gray and the water falling around them. "That wasn't foolish," he said gruffly.

She bit her lip and shrugged, feeling self-conscious. "Well, anyway being prone to diving into things like that made it hard when I got a nice, hard slap from reality. No fairy tales for me. No engagement, no chance for kids. I thought I got past it. Then I met you and, well, I got a little freaked out about things again."

She looked up at him, wondering if she could say what was in her heart next. As she was pondering, he gave her a reprieve. "I'm not going anywhere. And stop saying you can't have kids. You can't get pregnant, but you can have kids. There's more than one way to make that happen."

His words were fierce, his eyes locked to hers. Tears pressed against her eyes, and her breath caught in her throat. "Oh." That's all she managed before she burst into tears.

He wrapped her in his arms, and she just cried and cried. By the time she came up for air, she felt washed clean inside, the bundle of sadness she'd tucked deep inside finally dissolved.

CHAPTER 21

Sawyer concluded he deserved a medal right about now. He was successfully keeping his hands to himself (mostly) with Violet sitting right beside him. After racing down to Delia's office when she'd called upstairs looking for Marley, Violet had basically incinerated him. Every time he tried to convince himself the chemistry between them wasn't as off the charts as he recalled, he'd get skin to skin with her and realize it was hotter than anything he'd ever experienced. After their impromptu shower and talk, Violet had explained she was there for dinner with her parents and invited him to join them. Deep down, he knew what Violet meant to him, so he figured he might as well get the whole meeting her parents thing done.

Rachel and Isaac Carter were quite nice and easy-going. Violet shared her mother's coloring, and her father's bold, funny personality. Dinner had been excellent as always, and Gage and Marley had joined them for after dinner drinks. Violet crossed and uncrossed her legs beside him, and a bolt of lust hit him. It had never, not ever, occurred to him he'd be so damn distracted by a woman sitting beside him that he'd have trouble focusing on the conversation around him. Yet, he had manners. They'd been drilled into him by his parents, so he was not about to go all caveman and grope Violet with her parents sitting across the table. When she shifted her legs again, her thigh brushing against his, he gave in and curled his palm over her thigh. Mistake. The second he touched her, his cock twitched. He quickly pulled his hand away and started rocking a knife back and forth between his fingers to keep his hands busy.

"It's so nice to meet some of Violet's friends," Rachel said, her words filtering through the haze in Sawyer's mind.

Marley said something, and Gage cracked a joke. Violet rolled her eyes and glanced around. "In case you haven't noticed, my parents are kind of worry warts. Ever since I moved here, they worry I don't have enough friends," she said with a soft laugh.

"Oh hon. Moving is hard even when it's good. We just like knowing you're settled now," Rachel added, while Isaac chuckled.

Rachel's eyes flicked from Sawyer to Violet. "And I can't believe you didn't mention you were seeing someone," she said with a shake of her head.

Violet's cheeks flushed. "Really, Mom? Could we talk about the weather or something?"

Isaac threw his head back with a laugh and then looked around the table. "How about you locals give us some pointers before our fishing trip? If the weather holds, we'll be headed out on the bay tomorrow."

Conversation carried on with Gage and Marley ably picking up the slack. Gage threw Sawyer a knowing look. Only Sawyer knew that Gage would notice he was half out of it. When Violet had introduced him to her parents, she'd hesitated when it came to saying what he was to her. Not giving a damn, he'd simply announced he was her boyfriend. She'd flushed cherry red, but she'd given his hand a squeeze.

A bit later after Violet's parents returned to their suite for the night and Marley and Gage were heading upstairs, Marley glanced to Sawyer. "Are you staying at our place tonight or…?" Her question trailed off as she looked between him and Violet.

Violet glanced up, a puzzled expression in her eyes.

"Oh, you didn't tell her?" Marley asked.

"Tell me what?" Violet countered.

"I'm staying at their place while your parents are here," he explained with a shrug.

Violet's eyes widened. "You mean…?"

Marley grinned and nodded. "His suite was the only room available. If you're wondering, he never asked me. He just volunteered to give it up and asked if he could crash on our couch. He's pretending like we have a spare bedroom and technically we do, but he can't sleep there right now, so he's on the couch. Gage is re-doing the closet in Holly's room, so she's in the spare room now."

When he looked back at Violet, her eyes had filled with tears. Marley grabbed Gage's hand and yanked him away. "My mom's gotta get home, so we need to get upstairs for Holly.

Bye," she called with a wave over her shoulder. Gage threw a wink Sawyer's way and ambled along behind Marley.

"Why didn't you tell me you gave up your room? You didn't have to do that," Violet said, her voice cracking at the end. She wiped at her eyes and almost glared at him.

"It wasn't a big deal. I knew as well as you did, your parents' chances of finding a place on short notice were slim. I also know there's pretty much no space for them at your place, so it seemed like the only option. I've got three places to stay here, but with my stuff at the lodge, it's easier to crash at Gage and Marley's. Don't make it into a big deal because it isn't."

Violet was quiet for a few beats, her gorgeous blue gaze searching his. She startled him when she threw her arms around him. He was relieved he was almost back to new with his knee because he stumbled a bit with the force of her landing against him, but he managed to catch her.

"That was the nicest thing," she exclaimed into his neck.

He leaned back and brushed her hair out of her eyes when she lifted her head. "Well, if this is what I get for it, I'll keep sleeping on the couch," he said with a chuckle.

"Nope. You're staying with me," she replied with a grin.

"I'd suggest you two get a room, but we're booked," Harry said as he walked past them with a tray of full wineglasses. "In the meantime, how about taking this out front?" He winked as he swept ahead and paused at a table to serve the wine.

Violet shimmied down, the feel of her luscious curves brushing against him requiring him to adjust his jeans so as not to make his rock hard cock obvious to everyone around them. She dragged him along behind her with a firm grip on his hand. They pushed through the doors outside, and Violet came to an abrupt stop. His momentum sent him colliding against her.

"Oh. Look," Violet breathed, gesturing ahead.

The rain had stopped at some point during their dinner. The light was in that in-between place of dusk, smudgy and silvery. The moon was rising behind the mountains, its light breaking through the lingering clouds and glittering on the inky water below.

His heart clenched, something about the soft warmth of Violet against him and the light made it feel as if they were suspended in time.

He slipped his arms around her waist and rested his chin on her shoulder.

She angled her head just enough to catch his eyes. "I didn't really ask if you minded staying with me," she said with a sly smile.

Without a word, he closed the distance between them and caught her lips in a kiss. "No need," he replied as he drew back.

EPILOGUE

iolet stared at herself in the mirror. Her dark hair was tied up in a slap-dash knot with loose locks tumbling all over the place. She had a tiny handprint in blue on her cheek. With a laugh, she splashed water on her face and scrubbed at the paint. As she dried off, she heard her name and stepped out of the bathroom.

"Over here," she called when she saw Sawyer closing the front door behind him.

"Where…?"

"Marley's out on the deck with Holly and Alec," Violet explained quickly, knowing Sawyer was wondering where Alec was.

Sawyer's expression cleared, and he turned to toss his keys on the table by the door and kick off his shoes. Walking to her, he angled his head to the side, tracing the area where Alec had patted her cheek with his small hand covered in blue paint. "You missed a few spots," Sawyer said.

His gruff voice still had the ability to send hot shivers through her. It had been over two years since she'd admitted to herself she was head over heels in love with Sawyer. In the intervening time, he'd settled into life in Diamond Creek. Sawyer had surprised her with a proposal one afternoon at work. In the midst of her blubbering yes, he'd explained her office was where they met, so that was the only place he could propose to her. The silly romance of the gesture had sent her into a fresh round of joyous tears. That same afternoon, he'd taken her to the home he'd been building with Gage and Garrett on a piece of property adjacent to the lodge. They'd moved in a few months later when the home was complete. It was a charming Cape style home. Her fondness for the style of home came from being raised in the Northeast where Cape homes dotted every nook and cranny of the countryside. Their home was situated on the hillside above Diamond Creek, nestled into a cluster of birch with a lovely view of Kachemak Bay to one side.

Only a year ago, they'd adopted a little boy. Sawyer Alec, who they called Alec, was a bundle of energy at just past one year old. Marley had come by this afternoon to drop off a new paint set for Alec to play with. Holly, the kindest three year old cousin a boy could have, had promptly settled in to show Alec how to paint. Hence, the paint on Violet's cheek. She glanced up at Sawyer, and her heart clenched. "Did I?" she asked.

"Uh huh," he murmured with one of his slow, devastating grins that sent her belly into somersaults.

He caught her lips in a kiss and slid his palm down her back to cup her bottom and pull her flush against him. When he drew back, the look in his eyes was decidedly wicked. Flushed inside and out, she shook her head and tried to corral the need running rampant inside. "Marley and the kids are right outside. You need to stop it," she said, attempting to look stern.

"Just giving you a taste of what's to come. Later," he said with a wink as he stepped back.

* * *

Sawyer leaned back in his chair and looked over at Violet. She was laughing at something Marley had said, her cheeks flushed from the breeze gusting across the deck. With her hair mussed and her eyes as bright as the blue sky, his heart gave his ribs a kick, something he'd gotten accustomed to since he'd met Violet. His gaze slid sideways to where Alec was napping in his stroller. They'd discovered he slept best during the day in a stroller, so they had several scattered about the house. It was easier than lugging one all over the place. Sawyer reached for Violet's hand, lacing his fingers with hers, and listened while she and Marley chatted about something to do with…hell, he didn't know. He was tired from a busy day at the lodge and wasn't paying attention to much of anything ever since he'd eaten.

Gage's plan to schedule hiking and other guided outdoor trips from the lodge had been a smashing success, so smashing they were now looking to hire guides on because they couldn't keep up with the demand. Marley's sister, Lacey, helped out a lot, but she was pregnant at the moment, so Sawyer had been taking on a few extra trips and today he'd taken a small group on a challenging hike up a nearby mountain peak. The group had been comprised of hardcore hikers, as such he'd had to push himself. Since leaving his career as a Navy SEAL in the rearview mirror, he found his training came in handy. He could hold his own with the best of them, but it didn't change the fact he was still tired at the end of a hard day.

"We're putting Sawyer to sleep," Marley said, her words filtering through his half-sleep.

"Huh?" he muttered, not realizing his eyes had fallen closed until he had to open them.

Marley laughed. "Time for me to go. Let me help clean up first."

Sawyer shook his head. "Nah. I'm fine, just dozed off."

Violet squeezed his hand, her gorgeous blue eyes landing on his, mirth flashing in her gaze. "You're exhausted. We'll clean up and you go shower."

"Do I need to shower?"

Marley rolled her eyes. "Not unless you don't care about the dirt streaked here and there. You're as bad as Gage," she said as she gathered plates from the table and headed inside.

Violet stood and leaned over to check on Alec, adjusting the thin fleece blanket tucked over him. Sawyer stretched and stood. "I'll put him to bed and shower," he said, unable to resist the urge to slide his hand over the lush curve of Violet's bottom. Seeing as she was bent over in front of him, it was the obvious thing to do.

She stood and turned to face him, one hand on her hip and her eyes twinkling. "You're exhausted. I'll…"

"You will not take care of everything. I might be tired, but I can handle putting him to bed." He dipped his head for a quick kiss and rolled the stroller inside, wondering why all parents didn't simply leave strollers everywhere. It made for much easier carting around the house.

Not much later, he walked out of the bathroom adjacent to their bedroom to find Violet propped up against the pillows reading a book. She was a hard-core reader, a detail he'd discovered when they moved in together. She usually had three or four books on the nightstand, not to mention an e-reader filled with hundreds of books. The soft light of late summer night filtered through the shades. He'd learned to fall asleep when it wasn't dark, a quirk necessary for living in Alaska in the summer.

He lifted the thin down comforter and let it

drift down over them as he slipped under the sheets. Violet glanced over. "You just can't help it. You have to do that every time," she said with a soft laugh.

"Yup. Can't help it. It makes the air fresh under the covers."

She set her book down and reached over to flick off the light, immediately curling up against him. He lay there in the smudgy light of an Alaskan summer night with Violet's warm, lush body tucked against him. He idly stroked her back and listened to her breathing settle into a quiet, steady rhythm. Knowing that Alec was sound asleep in the bedroom next to them, Sawyer felt a sense of peace and completeness wash over him. He heard a hitch in Violet's breath and rolled his head to the side to find her eyes open.

"Thought you were asleep," he said, his voice gravelly.

"I forgot to say good night."

She burrowed closer and dropped kisses on his neck. "Good night," she murmured against his skin.

Damn. Just when he thought he had some semblance of control, she went and showed him just how powerless he was when it came to her. "Vi, if you..."

Her head whipped up, her eyes gleaming in the dim light. "You're too tired."

Even though his body had other ideas, he could barely keep his eyes open. He slipped his hand into her hair. "I'm never too tired," he said as he drew her closer for a kiss.

Thank you for reading Crazy For You - I hope you loved Violet & Sawyer's story!

Up next in the Lodge Series is Jacob & Ellie's story in Just Us. Ellie makes Jacob promise her one thing: they can't tell her older brother about them.

A tech billionaire & a sassy heroine get stuck in Las Vegas together. One scorching hot night lights a forbidden fire between them.

Don't miss Just Us!

For more swoony & sassy romance, check out my website for the following stories: https:// jhcroixauthor.com/books/

This Crazy Love kicks off the Swoon Series - small town southern romance with enough heat to melt you! Jackson & Shay's story is epic - swoon-worthy & intensely emotional. Jackson just happens to be Shay's brother's best friend. He's also *seriously* easy on the eyes. Shay has a past, the kind of past she would most definitely like to forget. Past or not, Jackson is about to rock her world. Don't miss their story! Free on all retailers!

Burn For Me is a second chance romance for the ages. Sexy firefighters? Check. Rugged men? Check. Wrapped up together? Check. Brave the fire in this hot, small-town romance. Amelia & Cade were high school sweethearts & then it all fell apart. When they cross paths again, it's epic - don't miss Cade's story!
Free on all retailers!

For more small town romance, take a visit to Last Frontier Lodge in Diamond Creek. A sexy, alpha SEAL meets his match with a brainy heroine in Take Me Home. Marley is all brains & Gage is all brawn. Sparks fly when their worlds collide. Don't miss Gage & Marley's story!
Free on all retailers!

If sports romance lights your spark, check out The Play. Liam is a British footballer who falls for Olivia, his doctor. A twist of forbidden heats up this swoon-worthy & laugh-out-loud romance. Don't miss Liam & Olivia's story. Free on all retailers!

Sign up for my newsletter, so you can receive information about upcoming new releases & receive a FREE copy of one of my books: http://jhcroixauthor.com/subscribe/

6) Like my Facebook page at https://www. facebook.com/jhcroix

* * *

DARE With Me Series
Crash Into You
Evers & Afters
Come To Me
Back To Us
Swoon Series
This Crazy Love
Wait For Me
Break My Fall
Truly Madly Mine
Still Go Crazy
If We Dare
Steal My Heart
Into The Fire Series
Burn For Me
Slow Burn
Burn So Bad
Hot Mess
Burn So Good
Sweet Fire
Play With Fire
Melt With You
Burn For You

ACKNOWLEDGMENTS

To my readers. Seriously, none of my books would be possible without you! Laura Kingsley does her best to keep my writing up to snuff with her editing. In addition to creating fabulous covers, Najla Qamber even keeps in mind my favorite colors! Last but certainly not least, DBC rocks my world.

xoxo
J.H. Croix

ABOUT THE AUTHOR

USA Today Bestselling Author J. H. Croix lives in a small town in the historical farmlands of Maine with her husband and two spoiled dogs. Croix writes contemporary romance with sassy women and alpha men who aren't afraid to show some emotion. Her love for quirky small-towns and the characters that inhabit them shines through in her writing. Take a walk on the wild side of romance with her bestselling novels!

Places you can find me:
jhcroixauthor.com
jhcroix@jhcroix.com

9 781951 228293